Growing up in Cornwall, England, Barbara Whitnell had two dreams: to be a writer and to travel. She has managed to achieve both these ambitions. After leaving college and teaching at a small village primary school she went to work at one of the offices of the British government in Nairobi. Here she met her husband and after they were married, travel became a way of life.

Over the next twenty years, while raising four children, Barbara lived in Uganda, England, Kenya, the West Indies and Hong Kong. When the children were older Barbara began writing. She contributed short stories to several British women's magazines and her first novel, *Passport to Peril*, was published in 1975. Since then she has written eleven further novels, several of which have been published in the United States as well as receiving widespread critical acclaim in England.

Now that Barbara's husband is retired, they divide their time between a house overlooking the Fowey River in Cornwall and an apartment in London. They have six grandchildren.

THE FRAGRANT HARBOUR

All Sue Russell wants is a holiday in the sun. Hong Kong is the ideal destination — she can meet her successful brother's new wife and see their opulent home on the Peak. But even before Sue reaches Hong Kong a chain of events threatens to disrupt her plans. Why was beautiful Mali crying so desperately in that sleazy café in Bangkok? Sue can't put Mali's plea for help out of her mind, just as she cannot ignore the hostility between her brother and his wife, and the shadow of the powerful Wong family which looms over them all.

Books by Barbara Whitnell
Published by The House of Ulverscroft:

THE SONG OF THE RAINBIRD
THE RING OF BELLS
THE SALT RAKERS
LOVEDAY
THE CAROLINE QUEST
CHARMED CIRCLE
THE MILL COTTAGE

BARBARA WHITNELL

THE FRAGRANT HARBOUR

Complete and Unabridged

ULVERSCROFT
Leicester

First published in Great Britain in 1999

Originally published 1972 under the title
'The Ivory Slave'
and the pseudonym Ann Hutton

First Large Print Edition
published 2000
by arrangement with
Severn House Publishers Limited
Surrey

British Library CIP Data

Whitnell, Barbara
The fragrant harbour.—Large print ed.—
Ulverscroft large print series: general fiction
1. Hong Kong (China)—Fiction
2. Large type books
I. Title II. Hutton, Ann. Ivory slave
823.9'14 [F]

ISBN 0–7089–4325–X

Published by
F. A. Thorpe (Publishing)
Anstey, Leicestershire

Set by Words & Graphics Ltd.
Anstey, Leicestershire
Printed and bound in Great Britain by
T. J. International Ltd., Padstow, Cornwall

This book is printed on acid-free paper

1

Someone was crying.

Sue paused, irresolute, in the doorway, blinking in the sudden dimness after the glare of the street outside, a dimness that did nothing to disguise the smeared tables and the general air of seediness which hung over the room. It wasn't a child, she felt certain, though there was a certain childish abandon in the shuddering, disembodied sobs.

Indecisively she looked back over her shoulder, towards the street where the perspiring taxi-driver was preparing to change the wheel. The violence of the sun seemed like a physical blow, and she pulled a wry face at the choice that was before her; a hot, dusty, fume-laden street corner in Bangkok, or the misery-charged atmosphere of the café.

She would leave, she decided. It seemed a violation of privacy just to stand there, listening, doing nothing. But, as she turned to do so, a harsh voice spoke to her out of the gloom.

'Yes? You want something?'

Too late to retreat now. Sue peered again

into the depths of the little shop, where a small, squat woman had appeared from a bead-curtained doorway at the far end of the room behind the counter. She was smiling ingratiatingly, revealing a mouthful of gold teeth, seemingly unmoved by the crying that continued unabated behind the scenes.

'Have you a Coca-Cola?' Sue came a little way into the shop, but not too far. It was infinitely depressing — the dirt, the flies, that incessant weeping. She did not want to commit herself to it and only a raging thirst prevented her from leaving even then. Who could have believed that this place existed in the same city as the fabulous Royal Palace, with its colourful, curved roofs and glittering spires?

'Sure,' the woman replied. 'I call the girl.' She turned and shouted something over her shoulder in a harsh, guttural voice, with no sign of the smile with which she had greeted Sue. She looks like a squat, malevolent frog, Sue thought and shivered, regretting bitterly the chance that had made her wander into the café. She would never have done so, but for the puncture that had made the taxi lurch into this side street like a drunk with one foot in the gutter. She glanced at her watch. Thank heaven she had left plenty of time to get to the airport.

'The girl come soon,' the woman said, her smile back in place. 'You American? I like Americans.'

'I'm English,' Sue said.

'Say, I like English too.' The woman squeezed her bulk round the end of the counter and approached Sue. 'Velly good, velly nice, yes?' She put out a hand and touched her hair, and Sue, her skin crawling, recoiled. 'Velly pletty,' the woman said, smiling broadly. 'Nice blonde hair, yes? Good figure, yes?' She sketched a shape in the air with her hands, laughing in a conspiratorial way. 'Men like, yes?'

Sue felt she had seldom taken such an instantaneous dislike to anyone and was about to turn on her heel and leave when the bead curtain parted and a girl came into the room — a girl so lovely that Sue stood, transfixed. She was small and delicately made, as were so many of the Thai girls, and she had perfect features with a skin as smooth as alabaster. No, Sue thought — that's wrong. Not alabaster. That's cold and hard and this girl has the warmth of old ivory. With great natural dignity she was wiping her large, almond-shaped eyes as in silence she went to the cooler to fetch the can of Coke.

'She no-good dumb broad.' The older woman spat in her direction. 'Who she think

3

she is, hey? Some sort of princess?'

She spoke the word in the American way, Sue noticed, with the accent on the first syllable.

Without a word, the girl handed the can over to Sue, gliding towards her with the grace of a ballerina.

'Hey, what you think my English, Mem? Velly good, hey?' The woman had come even closer to Sue and was peering up at her almost coyly, her smile pushing her doughy cheeks upwards so that her boot-button eyes were almost hidden. 'Yankee soldiers, they teach me plenty.'

I bet they did, Sue commented silently to herself, as she opened the can and took a satisfying swallow of the ice-cold liquid. The girl stood with her eyes downcast, leaning against one of the tables as if her misery was too great to be borne unsupported. She was hardly more than a child, Sue judged. Sixteen or seventeen at the most. Ignoring the woman, she spoke to her.

'Is there something wrong?' In the face of such unhappiness Sue was conscious that the question was hopelessly inadequate and was hardly surprised to get no reaction. The older woman's voice grated on.

'She silly, dumb broad. She don' wan' husband. I find her velly lich man in Hong

4

Kong. He want her real bad — send money, send ticket. She say first yes, anything to get out of this place. Now she say no.' Contemptuously she flicked her fingers at the girl. 'Silly, dumb broad.'

'Perhaps she doesn't like him?' Sue suggested.

'How she know?' The woman's voice grew belligerent. 'She never see him. Maybe he velly nice man, very lich man.'

'She's never seen him!' Sue's voice rose in horror.

'Listen, Mem. We do things different here. Don' you make tlouble, hey?' Her tone implied that she had encountered well-meaning do-gooders before and thought less than nothing of them. 'She stay here, she starve. No work, no fam'ly. She not my daughter, see? Her mother die and I take her and look after her. This man pay plenty money for pletty girl.' She turned away and flipped a hand as if the subject were closed. 'Everything turn out just fine.'

'But to go so far away, to strangers! Aren't you afraid he may not be a nice man?' Sue looked at the girl again and was struck even more forcibly by the small, defenceless presence. 'She's so very young.'

'What I do, you tell me?' The woman swung round to face Sue, hands on her hips.

'Sure I afraid. I afraid we don't get enough to eat. Seven kids I got, seven kids and no work now the Yankees don't come no more. One more week I work in this place, then *boom* — whole block come down and new hotel go up. So how we eat, hey? You tell me.'

Sue was silent. She had been pampered all her life and she knew it. There had been good schools, plentiful clothes, holidays abroad, winter sports and summers in the sun. This kind of hopeless fight for survival was something outside her experience. She had never felt more inadequate.

'I'm so sorry.' She sounded ineffectual and hated herself for it. 'Things are hard for you, I can see that. But she *is* so young, and Hong Kong is a long way from home.'

'She not so young.' The woman's voice was hard and without sympathy. 'She can't get no job, she must find man.'

At this the girl, who had been listening passively to the exchange with downcast eyes, looked up at Sue.

'What's your name?' Sue asked her gently.

'Mem?'

'She don' speak much English,' the woman said. 'Not like me, hey? I speak English real good.'

Sue ignored her. 'Your name,' she said insistently, looking at the girl. She pointed to

6

herself. 'I am Susan Russell. You?'

Comprehension dawned in the girl's eyes.

'Mali,' she said, in a light, sing-song voice. 'My name is Mali.'

'That's pretty.' Sue spoke absently, thinking hard. Surely there was something she could do. She couldn't just walk away from this girl and put the whole episode out of her mind, any more than she could have ignored a kitten with a can tied to its tail. Money was the obvious answer, but she had left herself with only enough Thai currency for the taxi.

'Look,' she said, delving into her bag and tearing a page from a notebook. 'I'm on my way to Hong Kong too — I'm going to the airport now. So you'll have one friend there.' Rapidly she wrote down her brother's address and telephone number, checking it with the address-book she always carried. 'Now, promise you'll phone me when you get there. If you need any help, I'll be there. You may be glad of a friend.'

Mali took the paper and stared at it, a frown of bewilderment on her face. The woman gave a sneering laugh and added a few words of Thai.

'She no understand,' she said to Sue. 'Silly, dumb broad.'

But understanding had dawned and suddenly Mali smiled.

'Fliend,' she said softly.

'That's right. Friend. You can find me here.' Sue pointed to the paper. 'My house. You understand?'

Mali nodded, the smile now illuminating her lovely face in a way that must surely have taken anyone's breath away, Sue thought. Surely there had to be a bright future for her somehow, somewhere, away from these squalid surroundings. On an impulse she pulled off the bracelet she was wearing and handed it to the girl. She felt sorry it wasn't of much monetary value. She wouldn't get much if she tried to hock it — but it was, she reflected rather bitterly, a collector's item. One of her own designs, produced with hope and enthusiasm and a faith in the future, but never to see the light of day in the boutique she and Steve had opened together. That particular project had bitten the dust before more than the first prototype of the bracelet had been made and the thought still caused an upsurge of bitterness. Forget it, she told herself — let it go, both the thought and the bracelet.

'For you,' she said to Mali, handing it over. 'To show I'm your friend.'

Mali's smile grew even more luminous. 'I thank you,' she said simply. 'Is beautiful!'

The taxi-driver appeared at that point to

say that the wheel was changed and they could continue their journey to the airport. Sue said goodbye and repeated her entreaty that Mali should contact her in Hong Kong; but as she went on her way she found that far from leaving the unhappy girl behind, the memory of Mali accompanied her like a small, exquisite ghost, unseen but ever-present. What was to become of her? How would it feel to be young and friendless and alone in an alien culture?

Sue looked down at the pale line of flesh that circled her arm like a scar against the darker, suntanned skin. It was a pity she'd had no money — yet the old harridan would no doubt have relieved Mali of it before Sue had gone a couple of yards. As a pledge of friendship, maybe the bracelet was better.

And no bad thing, perhaps, to be rid of it, even though she had suffered a pang when handing it over. Better to have no reminders of Steve or the ill-starred project that had cost her so much, both emotionally and financially.

Looking back, it all seemed like a kind of madness. She'd had a good job, designing jewellery for a well-known firm in London, but her infatuation for Steve had blinded her to the folly of giving it up to go into business with him. They couldn't fail, he told her; and, because he was dark and handsome and she was in love with him, she believed him. She hadn't taken into account the gadfly quality of his interest that alighted on this project one day and that project another — or the roving eye that made it impossible for him to stick to any woman for long. Their business had failed and so had their relationship. There was nothing left now but a feeling of betrayal. Steve had used her — spiritually, physically and financially and she still felt the scars.

Would he even have noticed her, she wondered now, if she had not been left a little money by her parents, so tragically killed in an air crash while she was still at school? Thank heaven she'd had the sense to safeguard some of it. Not a lot — but enough to pay her round-trip fare to Hong Kong to see Ian. Funny how, even after all these years, the instinct was to rush to her big brother when she was hurt or unhappy.

Though not so funny perhaps. He was twelve years older than she and had always been almost paternally protective of her — doubly so when they were left without parents. Now, at age of twenty-five, she felt she had caught him up. They were both adults together and it would be great to see him again, particularly as she had never met his wife. Ian had moved to Hong Kong only six months before and had met Serena almost immediately. It had been a whirlwind courtship and marriage and Sue was consumed with curiosity to meet the girl who had caused the usually cautious Ian to act in such an uncharacteristically impulsive way.

From the photographs she had seen, she felt it was understandable. Serena was a gorgeous girl, little older than Sue herself — slim and dark-haired. Sue was delighted to see how happy they appeared. She had long thought that Ian should get married, and felt that this must have been more than ever true now that he had reached such a senior position in Hong Kong. The monolithic firm of Banstead Marvell, a by-word in the Far East since the best-forgotten days of opium trading at the turn of the century, demand a great deal of their general managers. She had no doubt that Ian carried out the job admirably, as he did everything; but a wife would doubtless be a great asset, particularly a wife like Serena who had been brought up in Hong Kong and spoke Cantonese fluently.

As she sat back in the plane and watched Thailand dropping away from her, taking with it all its filth and fascination, its squalor and beauty, she resolved not to look back any more. She would put Steve Morrison and all his works out of her mind; Hong Kong was ahead of her — an exciting enough prospect in all conscience. She had enjoyed her two days in Bangkok, being attracted there as much by the jewellery as by the architecture. It was, after all, both her hobby and her profession. But that too now belonged to the past. In that city she had given away her last remaining link with Steve — a symbolic act that signalled a new start.

The sky outside the plane grew darker. Dinner was served and rapidly cleared away. The seat-belt warning came on, and below Sue could see the lights of Hong Kong, a confused urban blur half-obscured by the wing. The plane dropped lower over the sea and turned in a circle over the city. They were impossibly near the roof-tops! Sue's heart lurched as she saw them below her, surely close enough to reach out and touch. They would never make it. They were too low. The runway was too far away.

But suddenly the lights were behind them and the backward thrust of the engines was pulling the plane to a halt. Excitement rose within her. They had arrived.

2

It was the tail end of summer in Hong Kong. Still hot and humid, it was the sort of weather that made the Peak, where Ian and Serena Russell lived, such a desirable part of the island — that is, until the cloud came down at certain times of the year and it was enveloped in a dank impenetrable fog. For weeks on end, they told Sue, the walls of the houses and apartments ran with water and clothes were kept in hot cupboards to prevent them becoming mildewed. But just then, with the sun blazing every day from a cloudless sky, it was a good place to live. It caught all the winds that blew and those fortunate ones who lived up above the city were grateful for the smallest of them.

In spite of the heat, Sue walked the length and breadth of the city. Local residents, both Chinese and European, had a jaded air as if the prolonged summer had sapped their strength beyond endurance. The crowds that filled the pavements and spilled over on to the roads ambled along like dream-walkers. It was as if, Sue thought in irritation, when they impeded her progress, they were walking waist-deep through brown Windsor soup. sheer exhilaration gave her feet wings and she found it irksome to adjust her pace to that of the majority.

Hong Kong was an assault to the senses. No picture she had ever seen had given her any idea of the impact it would make on her and she relished every new sight and sound that came her way. Even the smells, though not always pleasant, were exotic and exciting.

After days of climbing up and down ladder streets and wandering around markets she found great pleasure in simply sitting on the terrace of the house on the Peak, watching the harbour which was spread before her. She loved to watch the ferry boats zig-zagging like water-beetles across to 'Kowloon-side' as she soon learned to call it. There were the ocean-liners too, and the junks and the sampans and the walla-wallas, each vessel forming part of the grandest maritime pageant she had ever seen. And as the sun went down and the lights of Kowloon began to prick the darkness, first tentatively and then with greater intensity as the darkness increased, she revelled in the feeling of the sheer wanton extravagance of it all; the huge blocks of light, the soaring, blazing brilliance of the sky-scrapers. They seemed to scream out a message. Take no notice of the poverty and squalor you see during the day, they flashed. This is the real Hong Kong, the harlot with the heart of gold.

That poverty existed was without question. Sue saw plenty of evidence of it in her exploratory walks and she was aware that the sort of life lived by Ian and Serena, and now by her, was like the icing on a cake, the bubbles on a glass of champagne. Only a small minority in the Colony wined and dined and danced as she had been doing over the past ten days and only an even smaller one lived in the sort of house the company provided for Ian. She acknowledged the fact, but would hardly have been human if she had failed to enjoy it.

She had at first wondered if she and Serena were going to like each other. Serena had welcomed her pleasantly enough, but there seemed initially a certain smiling lack of warmth about her; a wariness, almost, as if she felt that Sue could be a threat. But, as the days passed and Serena relaxed, she began to take Sue's friendliness at face value.

'You know,' she said sleepily one afternoon when they were both lying side by side, close to the swimming-pool. 'You know, I was terrified of meeting you. Ian's done nothing but sing your praises, ever since we met.'

'Oh Lord, how awful!' Sue was genuinely

horrified. 'I *am* sorry, Serena. There's nothing worse, is there. If it's any consolation he went on about you in his letters too. I couldn't believe he had really met such a paragon.'

They both laughed. 'And now you know the worst,' Serena said. 'No paragon — just an ordinary, very lucky girl.'

'You've made him happier than I've ever known him.'

'Honestly?' Serena opened her dark eyes and looked at Sue searchingly. 'I hope so.' She was silent for a moment. 'I've often thought,' she went on, 'what a marvellous childhood you and Ian must have had.'

'Well, yes — but not exactly at the same point in time. Ian is quite a bit older, as you know. He seemed grown up to me as far back as I can remember.'

'You were so secure though, weren't you? It accounts for the way you are now, I think.'

'How are we?'

'Uncomplicated. Trusting. Expecting the best from people and usually finding it.'

Sue raised her head slightly and looked at her sister-in-law, who was lying back with her eyes closed. She spoke in a dreamy, faraway voice as if she too were trying to project herself back in time.

'You make it sound just the teeniest bit boring!'

'I didn't mean it that way. Quite the contrary.'

'What was your childhood like, Serena?'

Serena was silent for a moment. 'A mess,' she said finally. 'I'm a quarter Chinese, did you know?'

'No, I hadn't thought about it.' That explained the blue-black hair and dark eyes, Sue thought. 'That must have been an advantage, in a place like this.'

'An *advantage*!' Serena shot up at this. 'Believe me, you couldn't be more wrong. My father was English, my mother part Chinese and part Portuguese, from Macau. In those days a half-breed wife wasn't exactly an asset to an aspiring government servant. Only a few years before he would have been sent home in disgrace, but we lived in more enlightened times. They merely blocked his promotion and treated us like social outcasts. It seems to me, looking back, that my childhood was one long struggle for acceptance.' She lay back and closed her eyes once more.

'It mattered terribly to my mother,' she went on, 'the fact that we couldn't join clubs — that we were marked as 'different'. Bruno and I — my brother, I've probably mentioned him before — we didn't mind so much. We had our friends, mostly Eurasian like ourselves, and by the time we were old enough to care there was a much freer atmosphere in Hong Kong. No one looks sideways now at a drop of Chinese blood. But then — oh then, things were different. My mother became almost pathological about it. Even when people were genuinely trying to be friendly, she thought they were patronising her. She tried so hard to be one of the government wives, yet she despised them at the same time. It didn't make for a particularly happy home life.'

'Thank heaven things have changed.'

'Yes, thank heaven. Young Englishmen openly live with Chinese girls now and no one turns a whisker. Not even the Hong Kong and Shanghai Bank, and that's an even stuffier institution than the government.'

'Where are you parents now?'

'They retired to Portugal. Bruno's staying with them at the moment, so I should hear up-to-date news of them when he gets back. Personally, I think they're crazy. They've moved into a sort of expatriate colony that's filled with people who've lived overseas all their lives and can't settle anywhere — just the sort of people they were with here and despised so much. Still, they seem to be happy — or as happy as they are likely to be anywhere. So you can see why I appreciate the serenity of life with Ian.'

The friendliness between them grew. Serena thought Sue slightly dotty for wanting to walk everywhere — she, personally, would not put a foot to the ground if not strictly necessary — while Sue felt that she would have gone out of her mind with boredom had she spent so many hours at the hairdresser or beautician as Serena did. Sometimes they went shopping together, and Serena was inclined to grow impatient and embarrassed when Sue fell into conversations with strangers — a tourist on the ferry or a shopgirl or a housewife in the taxi queue. Sue gave to every beggar that crossed her path; Serena swept past them impatiently, saying, rightly, that no one should be in need in Hong Kong. There were services to help the destitute, paid for out of taxes. Sue was being taken for a sucker.

Sue admitted that common sense was on Serena's side. Maybe she was guilty of moral cowardice. Maybe her alms-giving was more for her own benefit than the recipients. She was totally unable to analyse the problem and continued to drop her cents into the outstretched bowls.

Whatever their differences in outlook, Sue liked Serena more and more and had nothing but admiration for her ability to cope with the social demands of Ian's job, which were many. Ah Fung, the cook, was excellent; but it was more than good food that made their dinner-parties such a success. A lot of efficient organisation went into the mixture of guests, the seating plan, even the direction the conversation should take. No one was allowed to feel left out. Sue watched Serena at work and gave her full marks.

'You chose well,' she said to Ian one evening when they stood on the terrace together, leaning on the wall overlooking the harbour. 'Serena's a girl in a million.'

'You hardly need to tell me.'

'The job's quite something too, isn't it. You've done well, Ian.'

'Not bad, maybe.'

'Oh, the modesty of it!'

Ian laughed. 'I can't expect anything more in the way of promotion for quite a while, though. The chairman was out from London only the other day and hinted that eventually there would be a seat on the board for me — but I gather that 'eventually' was the operative word. At thirty-seven, the old buffers in London seem to regard me as a reasonably bright but still unpredictable and juvenile.'

'So you'll just have to go on slumming it here!'

Together they turned and surveyed the terrace with its tubs of bright flowers, the immaculate wrought-iron furniture, the steps leading down to the kidney-shaped pool, the graceful lines of the house. They caught each other's glance and giggled.

'Could be worse, couldn't it?' Ian remarked lightly, then, his tone changing, 'How about you, Sue? Is everything OK?'

'In what way? Financially or emotionally?'

'Both. I gather you caught a cold over this business venture of yours.'

'Double pneumonia, more like. I'm all right though, honestly. Oh, I'm mad about losing the money — it was such a waste! If I were going to blue it, I could think of a thousand ways that would have been more fun. But I'm young and I'm talented — I am, Ian, really — and I can get other jobs.'

'I don't doubt it.' He smiled at her, his rather beaky face alight with affection, and Sue thought, not for the first time, how nice-looking he had become. He had never been handsome, but maturity suited him and happiness had given him a warmth that was particularly attractive. 'And emotionally?'

'Equally impoverished, I'm afraid.'

'A temporary affliction.'

'I certainly hope so.'

'I'm sure of it. You're too warm and

outgoing to be that way for long — not to mention being, shall we say, reasonably comely?'

'Serena has been trotting out one eligible man after another, bless her heart, but it's all wasted. I'm not ready to get involved just yet.'

'Just have fun. Let nature take its course.'

And it *was* fun, there was no denying — the parties, the sailing trips, the beach barbecues. She could feel herself growing less weighed down by care every day, but each time she mentioned anything about her departure date both Serena and Ian begged her to stay. She was no trouble, they said. They loved having her. What was the hurry?

All too easily she was persuaded. She wondered sometimes if she would ever want to work again, she was adapting so naturally to this lotus-eating life, spending hours by the pool doing nothing more arduous than perfecting her sun-tan. It was over three weeks since her arrival and imperceptibly she was growing more indolent. The heat was getting to her and she no longer walked so much.

She was alone by the pool one afternoon. Serena had gone to the hairdressers and she had taken a book down with her, with every intention of reading it, under the shade of the huge umbrella. But even this was too much effort. She simply lay there, feeling the warmth soak into her bones, utterly at peace, more than half asleep. She was unaware of anyone approaching her until a voice spoke to her, very close at hand.

'Well, I declare. Sleeping beauty, minus the odd cobweb or two.'

Sue opened her eyes and raised herself on her elbows. In front of her was a dark, good-looking man, slim and tanned. He was dressed in cream-coloured slacks and a navy shirt, opened to reveal an expanse of brown skin and a silver medallion on his chest. There was something very familiar about his smile.

She blinked at him, still feeling more than half asleep.

'You must be Bruno,' she said at last, the penny suddenly dropping.

He pulled up a chair beside her and disposed his elegant length upon it. 'You have, as they say, the advantage of me.'

'Oh, I'm Sue. Ian's sister.'

'Well, how very nice! We're practically related.' He smiled at her in an intimate, appraising way. 'Cigarette?'

'I don't, thanks.'

He lit one for himself with a slim, gold

lighter and drew the smoke down into his lungs, looking at her admiringly. 'Fond as I am of my dear sister,' he said, 'this is a delightful surprise. I thought I would find her here, not a beautiful unknown.'

'She didn't know you were coming, did she?'

'No. I suddenly got homesick. I began to droop and die in Portugal. I needed the sort of charge that Hong Kong gives me — I get high just at the sight of all this.' Expansively he waved his arm, indicating the bustling panorama spread before them. 'Look at it — the Fragrant Harbour. Did you know that's what Hong Kong means?'

Sue nodded. 'I had heard.'

'Have you come to live here, or just for a holiday?'

'Just a holiday.'

'Enjoying it?'

'Very much.'

'And how about that sister of mine? Is she behaving herself?'

Sue laughed. 'Impeccably. She's at the hairdresser's at the moment.'

'She doesn't change, does she? I might have known she would be engaged in some such activity — being pummelled or enamelled or manicured or blow-dried.' He stretched luxuriously. 'Oh God, it's good to be back. The Fragrant Harbour,' he repeated, as if to himself. He drew a deep breath. 'You can smell the money from here, can't you? There's no scent like it.'

'Whatever it is, it's exciting.'

'The most exciting place in the world.'

'What do you do here?'

Bruno grinned down at her. 'Enjoy myself — what else?'

'For a living?'

'Oh, that!' He tipped his hand one way and then the other. 'Import — export. A little bit of this and a little bit of that. But I'm on holiday for the next few days. I refuse even to think about work. Do you like sailing?'

'To be honest,' Sue said, 'not a lot. All that lee-hoing, and leaning backwards over ten-foot waves. I don't seem to have much natural talent.'

'Hmm.' His eyes had that look in them again. 'I could say your talents obviously lie in other directions, but that would be crass, wouldn't it? I prefer to be more subtle than that — to hone my compliments to a fine edge, slowly and with care.'

Sue laughed back at him, unable to withstand so much high-powered maleness. He was obvious, of course. He loved himself to death, that was clear. But there was an

25

exuberance about him that was undoubtedly attractive.

'Here comes Serena,' she said, almost with relief.

He turned and lifted a hand to his sister as she came down the steps towards them, trailing a hand on the balustrade.

'Why Bruno,' she said coolly. 'I wasn't expecting you for a few days yet.'

'Darling, I couldn't keep away.' He got up as she drew nearer and hugged her, kissing the cheek that she presented to him. He held her by the shoulders for a few seconds, studying her expression.

'So what's with you?' he said finally. 'Aren't you pleased to see me?'

'Of course I am!' Serena patted him lightly on the cheek, and Bruno looked at her quizzically, his head on one side.

'You're not nearly as nice as your sister-in-law, do you know that?'

'Sue has no discrimination,' Serena said, taking the chair that Bruno vacated. 'She talks to anyone. Draw up another chair, Bruno, and tell me everything. How are the parents?'

Before he could answer, Sue go to her feet. 'I think I'll go and change,' she said, tactfully wishing to remove herself.

'That would be a crime.' Bruno's eyes were

on her again, and suddenly she was uncomfortably and, quite uncharacteristically, aware of the brevity of her bikini.

'I asked Ah Fung to bring some tea,' Serena said. 'He'll be here in a minute.'

'For three, I trust?' Bruno lifted an eyebrow at her.

'Yes, I saw your car outside.'

'Even so, I think I'll change.' Sue bent to pick up her towel. 'I shan't be a moment.'

It was something of a relief to walk away and leave the other two behind. There was a strange awkwardness about the meeting of Serena and Bruno and she felt they would be more at ease on their own. Perhaps Serena didn't appreciate surprises. She wished, herself, that she had been forewarned of Bruno's arrival, though nothing would have prepared her for the impact of his presence. Instinctively she felt she wouldn't trust him as far as she could throw him; but it was impossible not to feel a quickening of the pulses, for all that. In a way it was reassuring. It proved, at least, that she was beginning to unfreeze.

By the time she had changed into a dusty pink sundress and had brushed her hair until it shone she found that Ian had come home unusually early from the office and was drinking tea by the pool with the others.

'Hey, you're early,' Sue called as she approached them. 'Have they fired you at last?'

'No, so far I'm spared. I'd kept the afternoon free for the chairman of Consolidated Properties who was supposed to be flying in from Los Angeles, but his plane was delayed. Instead I'll have to see him tonight, I'm afraid, as his time is very limited.' He put his cup down on its saucer and looked across at Serena. 'The thing is, darling, he's bringing his wife.'

Serena pulled a face at him. 'And you want me to go with you and keep her occupied while you two talk business?'

' 'Fraid so. Do you mind very much? It shouldn't be a late evening.'

'What's she like?'

'I haven't the foggiest — but Eckberg is vurry, vurry American and vurry, vurry Puritanical. He drinks decalorised Coke and refers to her as 'Mother', so prepare for the worst.'

'Sounds like a really fun evening,' remarked Bruno. 'What does Sue do while all this debauchery is going on?'

'Oh, I'll be perfectly all right here. There's a good film on the box tonight.'

'Do your good deed for the day and have dinner with me.' Bruno looked across at her, watchful and smiling.

'Well thank you, that would be very nice.' At her ready agreement, Sue sensed rather than saw Serena look at her quickly and as quickly look away again. She was minutely studying her nails with pursed lips when Sue glanced at her. Whether her slight frown was on account of Sue's dinner date, or the fact that her nail-polish was chipped, was impossible to guess.

'That's great. I'll book a table at the Café d'Amigo and pick you up around eight — which reminds me, Serena, I hear you're throwing a bit of a party yourself tomorrow.'

'My, my, you don't waste much time, do you? News travels in this place like a bush-fire.'

'You'll come, of course,' Ian said. 'It's mostly business people, but there'll be a sprinkling of friends. I've been meaning to tell you, Serena, I've asked Neil Marriner.'

'Oh *no!*' Serena looked aghast. 'Oh darling, I wish you hadn't.'

'Why not? He seems a very nice chap.'

'Who is he?' Sue asked, feeling that the name was vaguely familiar and that she should know the answer.

'He writes in the 'Gazette' every day — you

know, 'Marriner's Log' they call it. You were laughing at it the other day.'

'So I was. What's wrong with him, then?'

'Well, nothing. It's just that we've asked the Wongs and he and Paul Wong had an almighty row on television during a chat-show once, not long before you came, Ian.'

Sue raised her eyebrows. 'Have I met Paul Wong?'

'No, I don't think you have. He's immensely rich. His wife runs that terribly expensive dress shop in Ocean Terminal, Sue — you know the one, don't you? We went there the other day.'

'Doesn't she prefer to call it a salon?' Ian looked amused. 'She's a force to be reckoned with, is Marsha. Paul is very rich, very powerful and extremely odious, but for my sins I have to keep on good terms with him, business-wise.'

'Then asking Neil Marriner to the same party wasn't at all wise.'

'What was the row about?'

'Heavens knows! Workmen's compensation or factory conditions, or one or other of the things that Marriner is always rabbitting on about. I can't say I like Paul Wong personally, but I can't see how things can be so bad when men are literally lining up outside his factory gates for work. Would they do that if he were a sort of latter day Simon Legree?'

'Marsha tells me she never sees you these days,' Bruno said.

'What nonsense! We meet all the time at various functions.'

'That wasn't exactly what she meant. There was a time, back in the days when you worked for her, when you were in each other's pockets.'

'You worked for Marsha Wong?' Ian looked across at his wife, his eyebrows raised in amazement. 'You never mentioned that.'

'I didn't really work for her — just modelled occasionally at the odd fashion show.' The look that Serena directed at her brother was far from friendly and his smile grew broader.

'How did Neil Marriner upset her husband?' Sue asked.

'They were on some sort of panel together — this was early in the year, Ian, before you came — and Marriner was going on and on about factory conditions and workmen's compensation, the way he does. He didn't exactly mention Paul Wong's factories outright, but the implications were obvious and finally Paul lost his rag completely. I gather he's never forgiven Marriner for it and everyone is terribly careful to keep them well away from each other.' She sighed heavily. 'I

31

wish you hadn't asked him, Ian.'

'Don't worry so much, darling. They're both adults, after all. I can't see the Waterford crystal flying — Neil Marriner is far too level-headed.'

Serena snorted. 'I know why you like him!' She turned to Sue. 'He interviewed Ian soon after he took over here and waxed quite lyrical over all the enlightened ideas he had for Banstead Marvell. He said that Ian made the unacceptable face of capitalism look like the runner-up to Miss World.'

She laughed. 'I rather like that.'

'I'm always so careful about who goes with whom — or is it whom goes with who?'

'Darling, stop *worrying*! I'm sorry about it, but it's done now. After all, there'll be dozens of other people to dilute them.'

Serena sighed heavily again, but had no alternative but to accept the position.

'It's a shame,' Sue said later to Bruno over dinner. 'Serena arranges things with such care. Still, I suppose Ian wasn't to know.'

Bruno looked amused. 'Strictly between you and me, I think there's a lot your brother doesn't know.'

'About what?'

He lifted his wine-glass and sipped

deliberately before replying. 'Oh, this and that,' he said at last.

'You like your little mysteries, don't you?' Sue was annoyed with him and he reached across the table for her hand looking penitent.

'Don't be cross, I couldn't bear it! It's simply that Serena and I have always been two of a kind. It was us against the world, in the old days — but now she's purer than pure, whiter than white, and I don't mind telling you it bugs me somewhat. I can't resist cutting her down to size a little when I see her doing her grand hostess bit. But that's enough about my sister, Sue. Tell me about you.'

Part of Sue stood back in cynical amusement, knowing that he was a practised charmer going into action with all the big guns blazing. But he had the magical gift of making a woman feel that she alone was the one, totally absorbing object of his interest. You're a sucker, she told herself — a push-over for the old masculine charm. Don't you ever learn?

Steve! Of course — that was the memory that had been teasing her all evening. They were so alike, Bruno and Steve, both tall, both dark, both with that type of piratical charm that appealed to her, in spite of

33

common-sense considerations that sent out warning signals to every nerve-end. Did one really always fall for the same kind of person, she mused? A recipe for disaster, if ever she'd heard one.

When he kissed her good-night ('I've been wanting to do that all evening. God, you're so lovely!' It sounded like a much-used line and Sue smiled to herself) she responded, but coolly. I don't think so, my friend, she thought to herself as she ascended the stairs to her room. Which is not to say, her thoughts continued, that you are not quite a dish. She smiled at her own confusion and went over to the window, pulling aside the light curtains to lean her forehead against the cool glass and look yet again on the glittering, sparkling jungle below her.

A jungle, that's what it was, she thought, the word catching at her imagination, and suddenly saw it as just that, with people everywhere clawing, clawing in a struggle for existence. People crammed eight to a room in high-rise blocks; people in shanties and cock-lofts and rocking in the foetid air of the junks moored in the harbour.

Not for the first time she thought of Mali. What had happened to the girl, she wondered? She had never phoned, but perhaps that was a good sign. Perhaps, after all, she had found kindness and friends and a loving home. She was out there somewhere, that was certain. Somewhere in the jungle.

3

The house on the peak was quietly pulsating with the keyed-up energy that preceded any of Serena's parties. There was no panic. Everything had been organised days ago and the servants slipped effortlessly into the party routine that was by this time, after months of Serena's rigorous drilling, second nature to them. They were aware that everything had to be perfect. The drinks had to be ice-cold, the buffet-supper piping hot; ashtrays and guest-towels had to be supplied in abundance; dishes of nuts and cigarette-boxes had to be filled and placed at strategic points. Ah Fung stood and surveyed the scene with critical, narrowed eyes. All seemed to be prepared. Missee would have nothing to reproach him with.

Upstairs Sue was trying to reach a decision. What should she wear? The white chiffon was cool and comfortable and looked marvellous against her tan, but she must have worn it a dozen times since coming to Hong Kong. Perhaps the kingfisher-blue Thai silk? Or the peach-coloured halter-neck? If she stayed much longer, she would need several

36

more evening-dresses, that was certain. She riffled through her wardrobe and sighed. Decisions, decisions!

★   ★   ★

Over on the other side of the island Mali too was reaching a decision — to try to leave the room now, or to wait until that strange, dead time of the evening before eight thirty when the whole house seemed to hold its breath in anticipation of the night's business. If she waited, she ran the risk that the man with the key might remember that he had neglected to lock the door after him when he had delivered her supper-tray — yet she dared not risk it yet. There were still noises downstairs; the slamming of a door, high-pitched peals of laughter, a carpet-sweeper droning in a deceptively cosy sort of way. She would wait.

It could only have been an accident that he forgot to lock the door. She could hardly believe it when she realised that he had merely closed it behind him and that the tell-tale scrape of the key in the lock had been missing. For over a week now, ever since her arrival in Hong Kong, she had been a prisoner, numbed by misery and despair. At first she had wanted to kill herself. All her life she had fought against a fate like this, determined not to sink into the same sort of degradation that had brutalised the woman who called herself her guardian. Guardian! Mali's lips twisted bitterly. She had taken Mali into her home for one reason only — because she needed cheap labour to look after her children while she plied her trade among the Americans who came on leave from Vietnam — exhausted and sickened by war and none too fussy about the company they kept.

As Mali had grown and blossomed into the sort of beauty that excited attention, she had been under constant pressure to become a prostitute. The soldiers had left, but there were others. Tourism had increased in Bangkok.

For some reason she had never felt the least desire to give in, not even in the face of the most grinding poverty. Some odd, fastidious gene must have prevented her — either that or the fact that she hated her guardian so much everything she stood for had become repellent. It was this fact alone that had made her consent to the arranged 'marriage' in the first place, even though she had bitterly regretted her decision when the time came to leave Thailand. It seemed to offer the chance of a decent, respectable life. A home of her own, a family. Everything that she wanted and had been denied.

It had not turned out like that. She had been met at the airport by a man in a large car. His appearance was not prepossessing, but he spoke to her pleasantly enough and her spirits began to rise a little. When she arrived at the house and saw its grandeur, she was more puzzled than elated and quickly became frightened again when a hard-faced woman and the man from the car rushed her across the entrance hall and up a curving staircase to the room where she now sat and where she had been a prisoner ever since. They did not speak to her, but thrust her inside and left her alone, terrified, with the door securely locked.

The days that followed had been a jumble — a kaleidoscope of emotions and confused impressions that, she had suddenly realised, grew worse after she had eaten the highly-spiced food that arrived for her at regular intervals. She had sufficient intelligence to know that she was being drugged and thereafter ate only the plain boiled rice, flushing the rest down the lavatory.

For several days she had been left completely alone. Then in the early hours of the morning when her spirits were as low as possible the man who had met her at the airport paid her a visit. He beat her, quite systematically. Not enough to show, but more than enough to hurt her. And then he spoke to her.

She had been chosen, he told her — chosen because of her great beauty and, if she did as she was told, she would live a comfortable life, surrounded with luxury. What more could any girl want? She would be well-fed, well-dressed. She would have the companionship of all the other girls — happy and contented girls, he stressed. Surely she had heard them talking and laughing together, while she had been locked up, alone? And in return for all of this her only duty would be to entertain the men who came to the house. Rich men, they were — often very generous. What could she possibly find to complain about in that? What else was a woman made for?

And if she didn't conform . . . well, then there would be other visits in the night and more beatings. Ice-cold with fear, Mali huddled on the bed, hugging herself, tears pouring down her cheeks. The man looked down at her, a smile on his lips. She would give no trouble, he thought. She would be like the rest.

She looked round the room now. It was well-furnished, thickly carpeted, with heavy, gold satin curtains at the window. She had never seen such a room, still less anything like the pink tiled bathroom with its shining taps that adjoined the bedroom. Yet for all its grandeur she would trade it instantly for the meanest hovel in Bangkok. How much had they paid the woman, she wondered? How much was her life worth?

There was only one way out of this. The English Miss had said she was a friend and Mali believed her. She fingered the bracelet on her arm and repeated the telephone number silently. She had been worried about forgetting it in view of the drugs and so had not destroyed the paper Sue had written on, but she had hidden it somewhere where they would never find it. All she needed now was a telephone. And, rapid though her passage through the house had been, she remembered that on the left of the staircase she had seen an alcove, draped with velvet curtains, where there had been a chair and a low table, with a white phone next to a huge porcelain ashtray. The picture was stamped on her memory as if even then she had known how important it would be to her.

She forced herself to wait. The sounds gradually died and the house was wrapped in stillness — a silence that she knew would last until the scrunch of the first car on the gravel drive signalled the beginning of business. It

41

was now she had to act.

Hardly daring to breathe, her heart hammering, she opened her door and like a shadow slipped through to the corridor outside. They had taken away her own clothes and given her a close fitting cheong-sam and felt slippers. She was glad of these now as she moved silently towards the stairs on the thick, red carpet, noting in spite of her tension the gold embossed wall-paper and the red-shaded lamps.

Just ahead was the staircase. She could see only the top few treads before it curved away and for a second she hesitated. Someone might be down there in the hall, where she could not see. A laugh trilled from behind a closed door and she jumped nervously. Her mouth was dry and she licked her lips. Whatever the risk, she had to go on.

Cautiously she moved forward and soundlessly went down the first few steps, then froze as a door banged from downstairs. She could hear voices below her in the hall and she shrunk back against the wall, a hand to her mouth. Another door banged and there was silence.

A few more steps, and now she could see the alcove and the telephone, silent and inviting. So near! She stood for a moment summoning every ounce of resolution she possessed, then lightly ran down the remaining stairs and into the alcove.

She was not prepared for the fact that her hand was shaking so much it was only with difficulty that she could dial the numbers. She fumbled and misdialled on the second digit and, gasping with frustration, depressed the receiver-rest to begin again. It went down with a 'ting' that sounded so loud to her that she felt sure the whole household would be alerted, but a quick glance over her shoulder confirmed that she was still alone. The ringing tone seemed to go on for ever. Would no one answer it? Was the English Miss out, perhaps? But at last the phone was lifted and breathlessly, urgently, Mali began speaking.

★ ★ ★

Sue heard the phone ringing as she came down the stairs, dressed, after all, in the favourite white chiffon. Her shining blonde hair brushed her shoulders and she glowed with the sort of joyous expectancy that Ian, watching her from below, hoped she would never outgrow. It had seemed some time since she had looked quite so carefree. He would have given much for the opportunity to have a few well-chosen words with the man who had let her down so badly, but failing this pleasure he merely thanked heaven that at last she seemed to be recovering from the experience. In his opinion, Bruno was not the man for her; but, if he had anything to do with her apparent high spirits, then the best of luck to him.

He smiled at her and was about to speak when Ah Moy, the amah, emerged from the study at the other side of the hall and indicated that Sue was wanted on the phone. She went through to the study and picked up the receiver that Ah Moy had left lying on the polished desk.

'Hallo?' she said. There was no immediate answer and for a moment she though that she was being subjected to the much-ridiculed heavy-breathing routine. 'Hallo?' she said again, her voice a little sharper. 'Is anyone there?'

'Mem'. The voice was a mere breath. 'Is Mali.'

'Mali! How are you? Oh, I'm so glad you've phoned.'

'Mem, I most sad. Bad people here. Gleat tlouble.'

Sue's smile died. 'What is it, Mali? Where are you?'

'I in big house.'

'Yes, but *where*, Mali? Where can I find you? Give me the address.'

There was silence from the other end of the phone and Sue remembered with frustration the difficulty Mali had with English.

'Where is your house?' she asked again, slowly and distinctly.

'I not know, Mem. House velly big, near sea.'

'Give me the telephone number, then.'

'I not know, Mem.'

Sue took a deep breath. 'Mali,' she said forcing herself to speak slowly. 'On the telephone in front of you now there is a number. What is it?'

A second or two ticked by. 'Yes,' Mali said at last. 'Is number. But Mem, I not know English — *oh!*' her voice broke off and Sue could hear the sounds of a struggle and a muffled scream. Helplessly she called Mali's name over and over, until the receiver was roughly replaced and there was nothing more to hear.

She stood by the phone for a few moments, biting her thumb-nail, desperately worried. There had to be something she could do. Call the police, perhaps? But, without an address or a phone number, surely they would be helpless. It was not as if she knew Mali's full name or the name of the man she was supposed to have come to Hong Kong to marry. She felt certain they would dismiss the whole thing as hopeless, but it was impossible to stand by and do nothing.

After fifteen minutes of being passed from hand to hand she finally made her report, knowing from the bland tones of the man at the other end of the line that she was making less than no impact. And, in all fairness, who could blame him? But at least he said that a note would be made of the affair.

Far from satisfied, she left the study and found that already the party had begun. There had been an influx of guests and she could see through the sitting-room from the hall where she was standing, and beyond it to the terrace, where Ian and Serena were standing greeting people as they arrived. Bruno was already there, glass in hand, and several other people whom Sue recognised from the many other parties she had attended since coming to Hong Kong. She hesitated, conscious that her pleasant feeling of expectancy had evaporated completely. She was in no mood now for an evening of enjoyment.

'You look like a lady with a problem.' The voice came from the direction of the front door which stood wide open to the drive, shedding a welcoming light for those still to arrive. She turned to see a tall, brown-haired man approaching her down the hall. Her first reaction was to admit it — she badly wanted to tell someone — but she checked herself. No man on earth wanted problems poured into his ear in the opening seconds of a party.

'No problems,' she said lightly. 'I'm Sue Russell, Ian's sister. I don't think we've met, have we?'

'I would have remembered if we had, I assure you.' His eyes were clear grey under finely marked brows and registered interest as he surveyed Sue. 'I'm Neil Marriner.'

She took the proffered hand. 'I enjoy your column.'

'Thank you. I aim to please.'

'But you don't succeed with everyone, I gather.'

'What journalist can?'

They turned and walked slowly together towards the sitting-room.

'I particularly enjoyed your satirical soap opera,' Sue said. 'What was it called — 'The Sick and the Useless', wasn't it? Serena is addicted to 'The Young and the Restless', but I found your scenario infinitely more amusing.'

Marriner laughed. 'I must say I rather enjoyed writing that.'

'But you like to put in the odd bit of social comment too.'

'I slip it in when nobody's looking.

Entertainment is the name of the game, really, but I can't see how any journalist in Hong Kong can avoid the odd shaft of criticism here and there.'

Sue looked at him without speaking for a moment and he returned the look questioningly.

'Something is worrying you, isn't it?'

'You're very perceptive. Look, I don't want to bore you — but, yes, I am worried and I literally don't know what to do next. Ian cares about people, but I can't bother him tonight and anyway I don't know what he could do. Or you, for that matter.'

'Shh, calm down.' He took her arm and propelled her over to a corner, out of the mainstream of arrivals. 'Tell me.'

Encouraged by the quality of his attention, she told him everything from the time she had met Mali in Bangkok to the result of her call to the police.

'It's hopeless, isn't it?' she finished. 'What can anyone do?'

He felt in his pocket and pulled out a business card.

'That's where I live,' he said. 'Can you come for a quick drink and a sandwich at lunch time tomorrow? Say twelve thirty? I'd suggest somewhere more exciting, but there are things I'd like to show you. I think this could be very important. It fits in with a spot of investigation I'm doing already. Can you come?'

Sue nodded, taking the card from him. 'Yes, I'll be there. Anything at all, if it's likely to help.'

'Good. In the meantime I'd be grateful if you'd keep this to yourself. Don't say a word.'

'Not even to Ian?'

'Not even to Ian. Not that I think he's unreliable — just that I have a hunch that there may be a lot more in this than meets the eye. The fewer people who know about it, the better. OK?'

'OK. Now please come and have a drink — I've been horribly inhospitable, I'm afraid. By the way,' she went on, when they were both served from the tray brought around by one of the servants, 'perhaps I should warn you that Paul Wong is here somewhere.'

'I saw his car outside. If there's any unpleasantness, it won't be my doing, I promise you.'

'What on earth did you do to him?'

'I made him lose face.'

'I see.' Even Sue, a newcomer to Hong Kong, knew the importance of 'face' to a Chinese. 'It was a stupid thing to do,' Marriner went on, 'and the last thing I intended. But he refused to answer my

49

questions on this television show we were in together and ended up looking extremely foolish. There's no doubt I won that round, but it was a tactical error. He's a dangerous man to have as an enemy.'

'You care very much about social problems, don't you.'

Marriner smiled at her. 'Correction: I care very much about people. I'm sorry if that sounds corny and News-of-the-Worldish, but it strikes me as being the most important thing in the world and precisely what's wrong with men like Wong. They are totally self-absorbed. The people that work in their factories are there solely for their convenience — they're a work-force, nothing more. They aren't individuals, with loves and hates and personal problems.' He gave a quick smile. 'I'm sorry. I didn't mean to lecture.'

'I'm interested.'

'That's nice. So's your brother, I think. He's the best thing that's hit Banstead Marvell for many a long year.'

Sue's reply was interrupted by Bruno, who came up and put a casually affectionate arm round her shoulder.

'Well, good evening, my sweet. You've met our crusading columnist, then?'

Marriner gave him a measuring look. The words were spoken pleasantly enough, but there was a faintly condescending air about them that he did not fail to recognise. Sue felt annoyed. She had been enjoying the conversation with Marriner and resented the spurious show of intimacy from Bruno.

'I'd better go out and do my duty with the other guests,' she said. 'I've strict instructions from Serena to mingle — excuse me, won't you?' Gracefully she left the two men together, but was not surprised when she looked back a moment later to find that they had drifted away from each other. Marriner had joined a young couple she recognised as Banstead Marvell employees and Bruno was talking animatedly to a plump, middle-aged matron who seemed to be enjoying his badinage, judging from the giggles that shook her double chin.

The terrace was by this time swirling with colour and alive with conversation and laughter. Set against the backdrop of Hong Kong harbour by night, the most ordinary company would borrow some glamour. No one, however, would dare to refer to Serena's parties as 'ordinary'. It was a glittering occasion, with muted lights shimmering on gleaming hair and bare shoulders. In fact, Sue thought as she surveyed the scene, it would be hard to find a more glamorous crowd anywhere. The collective value of the jewellery displayed alone would surely run into many thousands of pounds.

Marsha Wong contributed in no small way to this sum. She was dressed dramatically in a scarlet cheong-sam of stiff brocade. Her earrings were two cascades of diamonds like small chandeliers and reached almost to her shoulders. No doubt she had once been one of the small, exquisite, flower-like girls in which Hong Kong abounded, but now, in middle age, her features had hardened and set. She looked, Sue thought, as if she had been chipped out of marble and then enamelled. Yet she was still a highly attractive woman with a radiant smile which she could flash with great brilliance when the occasion demanded. Of her husband Sue could at the moment see no sign. Instead, by her side was a youth of eighteen or so, who was introduced as Edward, her son.

Edward Wong was quite unlike any other teenager Sue had ever met. It was not only his short-back-and-sides haircut that set him apart from the rest of his generation, but also his dark business suit and his air of total self-possession.

'My son is going to Oxford next term,' Marsha told Sue proudly, after introductions had been performed. 'We are very proud of him.'

'So I should think! Congratulations, Edward. It's not easy these days to get into Oxford or Cambridge, I know. Which college are you going to?'

'Balliol.'

Marsha, as if relieved that she had unloaded her son and could now talk to her own friends, smiled vaguely and melted away, compelling Sue out of politeness to stay and attempt to maintain the conversation. It was not easy. Every opening gambit was fielded and blocked.

'You're not drinking,' she said at last. 'Let me get you something.'

'I don't drink.'

'There's orange juice? Coke? Ginger ale?' Desperation crept into her voice. 'Would you like a cigarette?'

'I don't smoke.'

'How very wise! I — er — don't suppose this is really your scene, is it?'

He turned upon her the full force of his attention.

'I find it amusing,' he said, without a smile. 'My mother appears to think that parties such as this should be part of my education. She is utterly right, though not in the way she thinks. I find it highly entertaining to watch the 'upper classes' ' — the words were heavily underlined — 'Disporting themselves. They seem to have no idea that they are an endangered species.'

'I don't suppose they do. I hope you find Oxford equally amusing.'

He shrugged. 'It's a means to an end,' he said indifferently. His gaze wandered away from her towards the end of the terrace and he stiffened slightly. 'Is that Neil Marriner I see over there?'

'Yes. What a nice person he seems to be!' She threw this in, knowing instinctively that he would disagree. By this time she regarded him purely and simply as a pain of the first order and felt sorry for all his fellow-students, at present ignorant of what was in store for them.

'He is a complete charlatan.' Edward's voice for the first time held a degree of animation and Sue looked at him in some surprise. 'He should be run out of Hong Kong.'

'Strong words!'

'I feel strongly!'

'I know he disagreed with your father — '

'That has nothing whatever to do with it.'

For the second time that evening Bruno joined her and Sue was guiltily aware that on this occasion her welcome was many degrees warmer. Edward moved away, obviously as tired of the conversation as she was.

'I need a drink' she said faintly.

'I'm not surprised.' Bruno took hold of her arm in a proprietory way and signalled to one of the servants. 'You, my sweet, are suffering from an overdose of the Wongs, an extraordinarily painful condition only relieved by massive doses of alcohol, taken regularly. Have you met the old boy yet?' He inclined his head in the direction of an obese Chinese with a larger cigar who was standing broodingly at the edge of the terrace. 'I wonder what he's thinking about. He's been taking inscrutability classes for years, you know — he's just about ready to graduate, summa cum laude by the look of him.'

'Is he really as rich as people say?'

'Beyond the dreams of avarice.' Bruno rolled the words round his tongue as if extracting the last drop of sweetness out of them. 'Why Marsha slogs away with her business, I can't imagine. She must do it for kicks — they certainly don't need the lolly. My God, where are the drinks? I shall drop dead from dehydration any moment. Over here, boy. A gin and tonic for Missee and a Scotch for me.'

The party swirled on. Sue caught the odd glimpse of Neil Marriner, but he seemed to be keeping well out of the way of Paul Wong and all remained peaceful. Supper was announced and the guests drifted into the dining-room to fill their plates and return to the terrace where chairs had been placed, strategically sited so that the view would have the maximum impact. She was pleased when Neil materialised at her side and pulled up a chair close to hers — less pleased when the man on her other side leapt up to offer his seat to Marsha Wong. Her husband was looming behind her and the new seating arrangement meant that now Paul Wong and Neil were sitting in the same group — a state of affairs that Serena would deplore. Unhappily, she was nowhere at hand.

Not that there was much that she, or anyone, could have done at this stage. To attempt to rearrange things would have been both obvious and clumsy. But no doubt Ian was right. They were adults and could carry off the situation without unpleasantness.

Her optimism seemed well founded as the conversation touched lightly on a recent theatrical production and the visit of a famous British star. Paul Wong seemed content to eat in silence and Neil said nothing that could be considered remotely controversial.

Then someone in the group mentioned a recent fire in the New Territories that had recently destroyed a complete shanty town and unwittingly it was Sue herself who put the cat among the pigeons.

'What happens to all the homeless people?' she asked.

'Eventually they will all be rehoused.' Wong's voice had an air of finality. The subject was dismissed.

'I wonder,' mused Neil reflectively, 'how much human misery is summed up in that word 'eventually'? How many old, sick people or families with tiny babies will spend weeks in the open or in over-crowded tenement rooms.'

'And you, of course,' Wong said unpleasantly, 'expect me to do something about it? Buy everyone new houses, perhaps?'

'I didn't exactly say that. But, since you mention it, it occurs to me that it might be to your advantage as well as the poor unfortunate homeless if you got together with the authorities to ensure that rehousing was hurried up a little. After all, there must be many of your employees among them. Won't it affect their productivity?'

'I don't welcome your comments, Marriner.'

'This is absolutely delicious!' Marsha broke in tactfully, but her husband was not to be deflected.

'We all know where your sympathies lie.

From time to time I wonder why you left Britain and the welfare state. Is it not far enough to the left for you, Mr Marriner?'

Neil laughed. 'Oh, I'm the most unpolitical animal,' he said. 'We shouldn't air our differences here, Mr Wong. You know my views about the rights of the workers, without boring the rest of the company.'

'What do you want, Mr Marriner?' Wong's voice was like a steam-roller, battering down all the obstacles in its path. 'A country ruled by trade unions, like your own? It's not that sort of thing that has made Hong Kong prosperous.'

Neil's smile had died. 'I don't notice too much prosperity in Oi Man Estate, or down Hollywood Road,' he said quietly.

A shrill burst of laughter from the shadows behind Marsha's chair made all eyes turn in that direction. It was Edward who had been there all the time, unnoticed by the rest of the group.

'You are both so amusing,' he said. 'The whole complex situation in Hong Kong is like one of those puzzles made of twisted pieces of metal that can only be disentangled one way. You both have your different methods and they both fail.'

And that, Sue thought, is a remark I trust no one will pursue. The prospect of Edward

Wong giving his solution to the problems of the universe had little appeal for her and she was relieved when Serena appeared and implored everyone to have second helpings. Neil took the opportunity to remove himself and did not reappear until she was sitting drinking coffee, Paul Wong having taken himself off.

'I'm sorry about that contretemps,' he said.

'It was hardly your fault. You tried to avoid it.'

'I was afraid I would say too much, once I got started.'

'Are things really as bad as that?'

Neil stirred his coffee. 'What would you say about a man who lost an arm in a machine — not through carelessness, just through lack of proper safeguards? And was then paid off with a minute amount of compensation that would hardly keep him in groceries for a month?'

'Aren't there laws about that sort of thing?'

'Oh, they're working on it. Things are better than they were, but too much is left to the individual factory-owner. It's rather a macabre joke, but do you know what Wong's biggest factory is called? Paradise Textiles, believe it or not! Some paradise. It's more like hell on earth for the poor bastards that work there.'

'Edward is rather an odd-ball, isn't he?' Sue said, going off at rather a tangent.

'Mm. An unlikely sort of son for the worldly Wongs. Look — Marsha seems to be making her way over here. I think it would be best if I pushed off. If I don't see you before I leave, we'll meet tomorrow.'

Marsha gave Sue her brilliant smile as she sat down next to her.

'Ian has been telling me about you,' she said. 'I didn't know you designed jewellery. What kind of things do you do?'

'Things like this.' Sue indicated the earrings she was wearing and Marsha leaned forward to examine them more closely.

'They're lovely,' she said. 'Are you planning to work here?'

'I hadn't thought of it.'

'Suppose I asked you to design for me?'

Sue was half turned away from her, putting her coffee-cup down on a table at her side, but at this she looked up sharply.

'You mean for you, personally, or for the business?'

'For my salon. There is a demand, I am sure, for well-designed, modern costume jewellery — something in between the expensive, genuine article and the cheap-jack junky stuff that one sees sold in every market. There seems to me no reason why the craftsmen that turn out such good stainless steel kitchen-ware shouldn't diversify a little and produce jewellery and I know for certain I could sell it, just so long as it's something chic and different.'

'I'd certainly love to try.'

The old excitement bubbled up again. It was just the sort of challenge that she found exciting.

'Good! Can you get to work on a few designs and let me see them? Something with an eastern flavour, perhaps? What I aim to do is to produce something unique to Hong Kong.'

'I'll make some sketches,' Sue promised. 'It sounds great fun.'

'Fun that could be lucrative.' Marsha smiled, her wide scarlet lips revealing even, white teeth. 'I shall not be ungenerous if you produce what I want. Will you get in touch when you have something to show me?'

Sue was a little amused at herself for finding the prospect of work so beguiling. She had, after all, been on holiday for less than a month; yet she could feel her fingers itching to take hold of a pencil.

However, Ian was a little dampening about it when they sat down and kicked their shoes off to mull over the party after the guests had gone. He was helping himself to a final whisky and soda, having soft-pedalled on his own alcoholic intake all evening. Bruno had stayed on too and supported Ian's views.

'Those Wongs would skin their own grandmother for a few dollars,' he said forcefully, if inelegantly. 'You'll have to watch her, Sue.'

'She said she wouldn't be ungenerous.'

'Hmm.' Ian looked unimpressed. 'The use of the double negative was probably quite deliberate. She won't be ungenerous, but she sure as hell won't be generous either.'

'Marsha's not so bad.' Serena spoke from the depths of the armchair where she had thrown herself in exhaustion.

'Then why have you dropped her like a hot cake?' Bruno asked.

'Don't be absurd. She was here tonight, wasn't she?'

'You know what I mean. You were as thick as thieves at one time, but tonight you hardly spoke to her. Did you fall out about anything?'

'No, we did not. For goodness' sake, Bruno, leave it. One outgrows people.'

Bruno looked amused, but said no more.

'I gather,' Serena said, 'that Marriner put his foot in it yet again.'

'Oh no,' Sue defended him quickly. 'There were a few words — Paul tried to pick a fight, but it didn't amount to very much.'

'Thank heaven for that.' Serena yawned. 'I think Marriner sees himself as the Batman of Hong Kong, fighting corruption single-handed. Oh, I'm tired. Ian darling, I'm off to bed.'

Ian smiled at her. 'I'll finish this drink and be with you in a second.'

'I'm going too,' Sue said. 'Good-night, everyone.'

She and Serena mounted the wide staircase side by side, pausing on the landing before they went their separate ways.

'It was a lovely party, Serena. Everything went beautifully.'

'And there really wasn't trouble with Paul?'

'Nothing worth bothering about.'

'Oh, I do hope not. I — I try so hard, Sue.'

Sue looked at her sister-in-law in amazement. She had never heard her sounding so unsure of herself, or seen her so exhausted.

'Go on, go to bed,' she said gently. 'You look all in.'

'I feel it,' Serena admitted. Her lips tightened as she looked at Sue. 'It's that blasted brother of mine,' she said. 'I wish to heaven he'd stayed in Portugal.'

★ ★ ★

In the big house on the other side of the island Mali lay face down on her bed. The man had not beaten her then, though he had handled her roughly when he had found her at the telephone, but he would be back, he had made that clear. In the night he would come.

So there was no help, then. Stupid that she had not thought beyond the phone call — that her imagination had stopped at making contact with the English Miss. It had not dawned on her that there was no way she could explain her whereabouts, until she had actually tried to do so.

Only one way of escape was open to her now. She sat up, pushing the hair out of her eyes, staring miserably around her luxurious prison. With a quick shake of her head, as if dismissing all hopes and all regrets, she went through to the bathroom and turned on the taps, watching as the water filled the shining tub to the brim, her hand resting on the cool pink porcelain. She stroked it sadly.

The bathroom was the only thing in her life that she hated to leave.

4

Neil Marriner's flat was small and dark and possessed the noisiest air-conditioner Sue had ever heard. It was at a lower level than the Russell residence in every sense of the word, but still managed to present a view of the harbour, broken up in this case by other tall blocks of apartments.

'The Ritz it ain't,' Neil said with a grin, suddenly seeing the clutter of books and papers and records through her eyes. 'But the San Mig is cold. Would you like one — or anything else?'

'Beer's fine, thanks.'

She watched him as he poured it, trying to reach some conclusions about her impressions of him. Serena had implied that he was a prig, a tedious do-gooder. That he was serious about exposing injustices couldn't be denied, yet his daily column had a lightness of touch that delighted her and there was more than a hint of humour in his mouth and the creases at the corner of his eyes.

He looked up and she coloured slightly, conscious that her gaze had been a little too intent. She took her glass with a word of thanks and moving a pile of records from a chair he sat down, a small circular table between them.

'To business,' he said. He reached for a folder on the table and leafing through it he extracted a sheet of paper and handed it to her. 'What do you make of this?' he asked.

It was a letter, unsigned, addressed to him at the 'Gazette', and Sue read it through with a frown.

'I write to you,' it said, 'because I believe you to be interested in the welfare of ordinary people Helpless girls are being exploited, while our noble Police Force stand by and do nothing. May I suggest that you look closely into the disappearance of Fanny Boonthanakit of Bangkok on the 16th May? She is one of many.'

'How very intriguing,' Sue said, when she had finished. 'Did you look into her disappearance?' She looked down at the paper again. 'Fanny Boonthanakit! What a marvellous name!'

'Yes, I did. And stop me if this seems familiar. She was a lovely girl — more than just pretty, it appears — and came to Hong Kong to get married. Her parents heard nothing more from her, but did nothing for

66

some time because they were poor and illiterate and didn't really expect to hear. Eventually, though, they became anxious and contacted the authorities here, only to find that the girl had never arrived — although they had actually seen her off on a non-stop flight. Immigration had no record of her at all. So I delved a little deeper and found that no fewer than four girls had been reported missing under similar circumstances during recent months. I've got their dossiers here.'

He handed a sheaf of papers to her and she leafed through them.

'You certainly haven't been idle,' she commented.

'No, but my unknown correspondent thinks I have. This arrived two days ago.'

She took the proffered letter from him, and in spite of her concern for Mali she smiled with growing amusement as she read it. 'Wow — he doesn't pull any punches, does he? I rather like 'posturing and swaggering before the television cameras, playing for popular appeal while neglecting the criminal exploitation of the under-privileged'.'

Neil laughed. 'He can turn a fine phrase, can't he? He should try 'posturing and swaggering' in a sitting position. It's difficult to say the least!'

'Have you any idea who could have written this?'

'None whatsoever.'

'He has certainly become disenchanted with you pretty rapidly! He has a forceful way of expressing himself, hasn't he?'

'You can say that again. I find the 'bag of wind' bit particularly distasteful.'

'You must admit it has a certain poetic cadence. 'A bag of wind, an empty vessel, a broken reed, a charlatan' ' She looked up at this. 'A charlatan! That's what Edward Wong called you last night.'

'Did he indeed?' Neil looked at her attentively. 'What else?'

'Nothing else. He just gave a sort of wordless sneer.'

'Charming! He could have written the letters, you know. He's educated enough.'

'What would you do if you found out that he had?'

'Lean on him very hard. Whoever wrote these must know a lot more than he's telling.' He picked up the letters again and shook his head. 'There's no clue in the letters themselves. Both typewritten on an ordinary, newish, run-of-the-mill portable, posted in Hong Kong Central. Nothing could be more anonymous.'

Sue sighed. 'It doesn't bring us much

nearer finding Mali, does it?'

'It may do. Sue, all these girls were exceptionally pretty and all were from the poorest of backgrounds. They all left their countries of origin destined for Hong Kong, but never, officially arrived here.'

'How is that possible?'

'Immigration officers can be bribed, I imagine.'

'And what happens to them?'

He slapped the folder down on the table. 'To me, it all adds up to only one thing. White slavery.'

Sue stared at him, open-mouthed. 'You can't be serious! In this day and age?'

'What's so marvellous about this day and age? And what else fits the facts? If any of the girls were ugly or rich, I'd think there might be some other explanation; but they're not. They are all young, all beautiful, with nothing worth stealing but their bodies. I'm certain that's what's happened to them.'

Sue swallowed convulsively. 'It's — it's monstrous,' she said. 'Mali was just a kid, Neil. We must find her.'

'Maybe she'll call you again.'

'Oh, I hope so! She was lovely — well, you know that. She was very small and graceful, with the most beautiful skin — like old ivory,

I thought. Poor little ivory slave.'

Neil slammed his fist down on the arm of his chair.

'We'll find her, Sue, I promise. At least she's still in Hong Kong, we know that. What I propose to do — '

The shrilling of the telephone interrupted his words and he leaned over casually to pick up the receiver. 'Hi, Jim,' he said. 'How are you? Long time no see.'

As his caller spoke, the relaxed air dropped from him and he straightened in his chair, his eyes fixed on Sue. He listened without speaking for a few moments.

'It so happens I have someone with me right now who could be very interested,' he said at last. 'Can you rush the prints round to me, Jim? Sure. Thanks, I'd appreciate it.'

He put the phone down and looked at Sue for a long minute.

'What is it?' she asked uneasily, a presentiment of doom making a shadowy appearance at the back of her mind.

'That was Jim Fairman,' he said at last. 'A mate of mine in the police — a back-room boy. I asked him some time ago to let me have anything he might get on missing girls, particularly outstandingly pretty ones.'

'And?'

He leant over and picked up her hand that

was nervously plucking the cover on the arm of the chair.

'This is an outside chance, that's all. It may have no connection with Mali.'

'What did he say?'

Neil took a breath. 'There was a girl fished out of Aberdeen Harbour early this morning. She was young — about sixteen or so — and very pretty. Jim, who knows about these things, thinks she looks more Thai than Chinese.'

'Oh Neil, *no!*' Sue tightened her grip on his hand.

'It's only an outside chance, Sue. Don't look like that!'

'He's sending the photographs round to you?'

'Yes, they shouldn't take more than fifteen or twenty minutes. I'll get you a drink in the meantime.'

Seldom had she needed one more. Common sense might say that the chance of it proving to be Mali was a slight one, but there was an inevitable feeling of fate about it all. Ever since she had heard the struggle on the end of the phone the night before, her fears for Mali had refused to be quieted.

Even so, a small flicker of hope still burned. That was soon extinguished when she looked at the photographs.

'It's Mali,' she said flatly. 'Not a shadow of doubt.'

'You're sure?'

Sue pointed to the girl's arm which hung over the side of the stretcher.

'If I had any doubt that would settle it once and for all. That's the bracelet I gave her. There's not another like it in the whole world.'

Neil took the print and put it in the file with the other papers. 'You understand what this means,' he said gently. 'I'm afraid you'll have to identify her.'

Sue looked startled. 'But I don't know her!'

'You know more than anyone else.'

'You mean, go to the morgue?'

'I'm sorry, Sue. You must tell the police what you know. She won't have died in vain if we get the whole thing out in the open, will she?'

'No' Sue bit her lip unhappily. 'No, you're right of course. But, Neil, it terrifies me.'

'The thought is worse than the deed. I'll stay with you.'

'When ought we to go?'

He looked at his watch. 'We'll wait until after two, when everyone's back from lunch. Which reminds me, I'm going to make you a sandwich and you're going to eat it.'

'I'm really not hungry.'

'No arguments!'

The minutes passed slowly until it was time to present themselves at Police Headquarters. They were shown immediately into the presence of a British police officer, a middle-aged man with a red, fleshy face and sandy hair. He rose to his feet and extended a hand to Sue as she entered the room, followed closely by Neil.

'I'm Chief Inspector Petter,' he said. 'You have some information about this girl that was found, I believe.'

'I met her in Bangkok,' Sue said, her voice emerging as a dry whisper. Nervously she cleared her throat.

'That's interesting.' Petter's voice had an amused ring to it and he was smiling blandly. 'Bangkok, you say?'

'That's right. Her name was Mali, but I'm afraid I don't know the rest of it.'

'Well, well. Most public-spirited of you to come along, Miss Russell.'

Sue felt a shaft of annoyance that he seemed to be treating the whole thing so lightly and her voice sharpened.

'She phoned me last night.'

'From Bangkok?'

'From Hong Kong. She came here to get married. While she was talking to me, the phone was snatched away from her and I could hear the sounds of a struggle.'

'*Most* interesting!' Petter's amusement was quite open now. 'You would, then, be surprised to learn that the girl's family have only this minute left here having made a positive identification, and that her name was — ' he picked up a buff-coloured file on his desk and consulted it. 'Her name was Winnie Leung Fu of Causeway Bay. Miss Russell, it's been said before and I'll say it again, all these Chinese look alike.'

Sue looked at him in amazement. She had been so keyed up for the ordeal of identifying the body that she found it hard to take in this new development, but as the policeman's words sank in her first reaction was one of incredulous relief. It wasn't true, then! Mali wasn't dead after all! Then she remembered the bracelet.

'But Chief Inspector, it *was* Mali! She was wearing a bracelet I'd given her. I saw it in the photographs that Mr Marriner showed me.'

Petter's smile died and he shot a look of dislike at Neil.

'Damned journalists! You had no right to see those. Be that as it may, Miss Russell, the girl's mother and brother were both in here not ten minutes ago. They had already seen the body and made the identification.'

Sue opened her mouth to protest further, but out of the corner of her eye she caught the slight movement from Neil. She glanced at him and he shook his head briefly. Dissatisfied, she subsided into silence.

'I came as a friend of Miss Russell,' Neil said. 'But journalists, damned or otherwise, can't help a certain amount of professional interest. Would you give me the full story? Did she fall or was she pushed?'

'It was suicide.' Petter's voice was decisive and dismissive. 'Open-and-shut case.'

'Was the family surprised?'

'Evidently not, at least not the brother. He knew that the girl had been having an affair with an American and believed herself in the family way. You don't need me to tell you what a disgrace that would be to a respectable Chinese girl. She confided all this to the brother and threatened suicide, since the American had skipped back to the States and left her on her own. He thought he had talked her out of it, but evidently not.'

'You said *believed* herself to be pregnant,' Neil said. 'Was she?'

Petter shuffled the papers on his desk. 'Well, no. Sad, eh? The girl was mistaken, it seems. The pathologist says there was no sign of it.'

'Yet you call that an open-and-shut case?'

Neil's voice was quietly incredulous.

Wearily Petter ran his fingers through his thinning hair.

'Don't blow this thing up, Marriner. We have enough real crime on our hands without chasing fantasies. There wasn't a mark on the girl. The report says death by drowning. The brother said she had talked often about suicide. For heaven's sake leave it at that.'

'Can I have the address of the family?'

'So you can hound them? No, you can't.' Petter stabbed a plump finger towards Neil. 'Leave it alone, Marriner. If I find you've been snooping, I'll see you never get another story as long as you're in this town, so help me. Now, if you'll excuse me, I have a large volume of work to get through today. Thanks again for coming in, Miss Russell.'

He picked up a file and after a second's hesitation Neil shrugged and raised his eyebrows at Sue, signalling resignation.

'But it *was* Mali,' she said stubbornly when they were outside. 'Why didn't you stick up for me, Neil?'

He waited until they were outside the building and inside his car before replying.

'That man had been paid off,' he said. 'I could swear to it. He's had strict instructions to hush the whole thing up.'

'But the brother he mentioned?'

'He probably existed — well, someone existed who claimed to be her brother. Somebody went through all the formalities and Petter has been paid off to accept it all without a query.'

'But he was a police officer — a senior man. The soul of respectability, one would have thought.'

Neil half laughed and half sighed at the same time.

'How can I begin to tell you about bribery in Hong Kong? It's a way of life, Sue. Less so now than it was, perhaps, thanks to the Independent Commission Against Corruption — and, God knows, I'm not singling out the police any more than any other section of society. But it's useless to deny that it goes on and probably always will. Look — ' he was serious now, speaking rapidly and very quietly, 'a young policeman comes out from England with a wife and kids perhaps, not realising that the salary he's going to be paid that sounds quite reasonable will hardly keep him in cornflakes out here. He could be straight as a die, and many stay that way, to their resounding credit — but there are others who don't. It's all too easy *not* to stay straight in Hong Kong, believe me. At first the pay-offs probably don't involve doing anything at all. The money just appears in his drawer against the day when he's needed. And then, perhaps, all he has to do is suppress a few traffic offences, allow a few lorries to park every night in forbidden areas. It must all seem very harmless at first.'

'And then?'

Neil shrugged. 'Well, then he's in their power, isn't he? Then they've got him.'

'Who are 'They'?'

'The big bosses. The Triads.'

'That's a sort of Chinese Mafia, isn't it?'

'Sort of. There's a great deal of enmity between different Triads, but between them they have all the vice-rings sewn up, be it drugs or prostitution or whatever.'

'White slaving?'

'Naturally. So it all fits, doesn't it?'

Sue lapsed into silence as Neil started the car and drove out into the bumper-to-bumper traffic of Hong Kong.

'So what do we do now?' she asked.

'We do nothing,' he said. 'Sorry, Sue, but I'm not having you mixed up in this, no way. You stay up in your little eyrie on the Peak and keep out of danger.'

'That's not fair!'

'These people are dangerous. I wouldn't want you to be found floating in Aberdeen Harbour one dark night.'

Sue compressed her lips mutinously and

stared straight ahead, saying nothing. Neil glanced at her and smiled.

'Don't look so mad! Just rely on me to go on digging. Somehow I'll find out who wrote those letters — that's the breakthrough I'm looking for.'

'You'll let me know when you do?'

'Of course. Maybe we could have dinner one night. I'll give you a ring.'

'You do that thing.'

She fell silent, depressed by events and strangely let down by Neil's vagueness about a future meeting. He dropped her at the house and seeing Bruno's car outside she went straight upstairs to her room, guessing that he would be by the pool with Serena and feeling disinclined for light conversation.

She kicked off her sandals and flung herself full length on the bed, staring bleakly at the ceiling. It was useless to tell herself she had no reason to feel guilty, that she had done all that she could for Mali. Reason had nothing to do with it. Somehow she had failed the girl and the realisation was a physical pain. If only she had said the right words — asked the right questions!

Useless to go over and over those few moments when she had heard the pathetic voice at the other end of the phone. Resolutely she got up. She would make an

79

effort, she told herself, to see the tragedy in a less hysterical way. Maybe it would be a good idea to join the others after all.

She looked out of the bedroom window which gave her a clear view of the terrace below and the pool below that. As she had guessed, Bruno and Serena were down there, lying side by side on the pool-side chairs, engrossed in conversation. They seemed to be friendly enough today, she thought, and was gladdened at the sight. She would leave them to it, she thought — give them time to sort out their differences and come to terms with each other.

But even as she watched, Serena stood up in one lithe, graceful movement, snatched up her towel and flounced away from her brother with a face like thunder. The truce, it appeared, was only a temporary one after all.

★　★　★

Bruno watched her go through lazy, half-closed eyes, smiling a little to himself.

'You've come a long way, baby,' he said silently to her retreating back-view.

He remembered so well the first time she had met Ian. She was going through one of her depressed spells, in the sort of mood when she felt lonely and insecure and unloved. Attractive though she was, she had not managed to meet a man both rich and eligible who wanted a permanent relationship with her. There were married men in plenty who indicated their willingness to enjoy a little on the side — and she wasn't averse to that. There was an impecunious engineer who wanted to marry her — which of course was out of the question. The perfect combination of all the desirable qualities necessary in a husband seemed to elude her.

Not that she had wanted a husband until quite recently. She had enjoyed her freedom and laughed scornfully at her school-friends who had rushed into matrimony straight from the schoolroom. But there were times, as the years went by, when security seemed an attractive proposition after all.

Then along had come Ian. She was quick to realise that here was a man, at last, who fulfilled all the conditions. He was single; he had a good position in Hong Kong; he even had a private income, or so the brother of a girl who worked at the bank assured her. Bruno had been her confidant from the beginning. Together they had conspired to dazzle Ian — yet here she was now, behaving like some romantic teenager.

He had merely told her that Jack Palliser was back in town and wanted to see her, that was all. 'He used to be pretty generous to you, didn't he?'

'Leave me alone, damn you. I'm a married woman now. All that's behind me.'

'What's to lose? I promised Jack I'd try to get hold of you. Ian won't know. You can borrow my pad for the afternoon.'

'Bruno, for the last time!' Serena's voice was tight with anger. 'I *love* Ian — can't you understand that?'

Bruno drew deeply at his cigarette and raised an eyebrow at her. 'There was a time when you described him as the best gilt-edged meal-ticket you were likely to find, remember?'

'That was before I really knew him.'

'How very sweet! Jack will be disappointed. You're an essential part of Hong Kong, to him.'

'You make me feel like a common little prostitute!'

'Oh never common, darling — and never more than an enthusiastic amateur.'

'Leave me alone, Bruno — and, what's more, leave Sue alone. She's not in your league and she's been hurt enough.'

Bruno drew at his cigarette again. 'She is, unless I am greatly mistaken, above the age of consent?'

'I said, leave her alone.'

He laughed. 'Darling, that is surely for her to decide. There's something about that cool, blonde, long-legged look that really turns me on.'

'She's no fool. She'll see right through you.'

'Just like Ian saw through you?'

It was this last remark that had caused her to sweep away in a fury. Silly bitch, Bruno thought, half-irritated and half-affectionate. Who did she think she was kidding? They'd been two of a kind once upon a time and not so long ago at that. It was too much to believe that she had changed.

There didn't seem much point in hanging around under the circumstances. Sue was out, it appeared. He looked at his watch and did some quick calculations. If he left now, he would be in plenty of time to get changed and meet that little Chinese dolly-bird from her office — the one he had been introduced to last night. What the hell was her name? Lydia or Linda or some such. He rose lazily from his chair, flung his towel over his shoulder and sauntered off, casting a casual look upwards at Sue's bedroom window as he passed the house.

'I'll be back, sweetheart,' he said silently, anticipation giving his handsome face a predatory expression. 'You can make a bet on it.'

5

With Marsha Wong's assignment very much in mind, Sue forsook the tourist beat in Hong Kong for her drawing-board and pencil. Every morning she seated herself in a shady corner of the terrace and it was as if she was inspired by the very air she breathed. The swoop of a junk's deck, the billowing curve of its sail, a sea-bird in flight, the ferns which sprang from the rocky crevices of the grey walls bordering the twisty roads of the Peak. All were grist to her mill and with this inspiration she felt satisfied at the end of a week that she had produced a selection of designs that were as good as anything she had done — designs uniquely her own, yet with a truly oriental flavour.

After considerable thought she had even incorporated the design of the bracelet she had given to Mali. There was no sense, she decided, in wasting a good idea and the feather design she had used seemed equally suited to this eastern environment where birds were such a feature of everyday life. One of the sights that most enchanted her was the morning parade of old men in their pyjamas, bamboo cages in hand, taking their birds for a walk. And so the stylised feathers were incorporated yet again and her feeling of contentment in a job well done was diminished as she thought once more of Mali.

There had been no further word from Neil, which was an undeniable disappointment, quite apart from the fact that it meant he had made no progress in the Mali affair. It was true that when they parted after the abortive trip to the police-station he had been vague about a meeting — yet he had mentioned dinner and there had been an immediate rapport between them. Still the call had not come.

She made a point of tuning in to his weekly broadcast and found it a matter of great satisfaction that he performed so competently and in such an entertaining way. He came over as a pleasant-voiced man, whose sensitive and rather idealistic outlook had a leavening of dry humour. It would be nice to see him again, she thought; but the phone remained obstinately silent.

At least it was silent where Neil Marriner was concerned. Bruno, on the other hand, was constant in his attentions and, because of his undeniable attraction and the fact that she had no other claims on her, she went out with him several times.

Now people were beginning to think of them as a pair and to invite them to functions together — which, as far as Sue was concerned, was a great pity since it had taken very little time for her to realise that in fact they had little to say to each other. Their conversation remained on the most superficial level. On basic principles they differed completely. Worse, Sue had no intention of being manoeuvred into bed with him and this was becoming more and more difficult to avoid, the more often she went out with him. The situation was becoming difficult and it seemed that some straight talking would soon be required. Meanwhile he called and phoned constantly. Thank heaven he had now gone back to work and was occupied at his office most of the day — though not too much occupied, it seemed. Protracted lunch times that went on until past three in the afternoon seemed the rule rather than the exception. Sue had been grateful to Marsha for giving her a good reason for staying at home.

She phoned her now to tell her that she had a good selection of designs to show her and made a date to call round at her house with them the following morning.

Her appointment was for ten-thirty. Marsha was a business-woman with a very busy schedule. Looking round the enormous

86

drawing-room, Sue could not believe that there could be any financial necessity for her to work, unless the acquiring of worldly goods had reached the point of mania. Certainly there was an abundance of beautiful things in this room alone.

Beautiful carpets were commonplace in Hong Kong, but the pale green one which covered the entire floor here was breathtaking — silken and delicately figured. Low rose-wood tables bore intricately patterned porcelain lamps with shades of palest Thai silk. Display cabinets were crammed with jade, ivory and porcelain in such profusion that the impact was lost — and there were more ornaments on the mantel over which hung a huge and, to Sue's mind, vastly over-ornate gilded mirror. A grand piano stood in the far corner of the room bearing a massive arrangement of white lilies whose cloying scent mingled with the aroma of joss-sticks.

Above her head hung a glittering crystal chandelier which would not have looked out of place in some ducal ballroom. Perhaps, Sue thought, money really did give off a scent of its own and this added to the airless atmosphere.

The house was built on the cliff just beyond Repulse Bay and long windows led to a terrace which overlooked a view every bit as breathtaking as the one from the Russell's house, yet totally different. This was the other face of Hong Kong; the still sea, the distant islands that seemed to float gently in the mist. Sue walked to the window and looked outside, noting the neat, formal gardens and the turquoise swimming-pool that was apparently carved from the rock.

'Good-morning, Sue. How nice to see you!'

'Oh!' Sue turned round with a startled smile. She had not heard Marsha approaching on the thick carpet and her thoughts had been miles away. 'Hallo, Marsha. I was admiring your view.'

'It's beautiful, isn't it?' She was smiling as she spoke, but her smile died and was replaced by a look of annoyance as Edward crossed the terrace in his swimming-trunks, a towel over his shoulder. He was heading in the direction of the pool and could not possibly have avoided seeing them both at the window, looking out at him. However, he did not acknowledge their presence. There was no smile, no friendly wave of the hand; just a small and strangely arrogant back-view turned upon them with an air of total disinterest.

'He looks very fit.' Sue's remark was to fill

an awkward pause. Marsha's gaze was riveted on her son and she seemed abstracted.

'Oh yes; he swims every day, though he doesn't care for sport.'

'When does he leave for Oxford?'

'In a week's time. I hope he . . . '

Marsha's voice trailed away and Sue could well understand why. There were so many things that a mother would hope for if she had a son like Edward. That he would learn to enjoy life a little more must have been one among many.

'And now, where are these designs you have made for me?' Marsha seemed to make a visible effort to dismiss her maternal worries and turned to Sue with her usual brilliant smile. 'I am so looking forward to seeing them.'

'I hope you won't be disappointed.'

The sketches were in a portfolio that Sue so far held under her arm. Now she opened it and spread the contents on a table which was set before a deep oyster-satin settee. Together they sat down and Marsha examined each drawing long and silently, her shrewd eyes smiling no longer. She looked cold and business-like and Sue suddenly felt unsure of herself — a schoolgirl again, waiting for exam results.

Eventually the older woman put the last

sheet down and turned to Sue, smiling again. 'I like them,' she said. 'I like them very much. They have just the modern, uncluttered look I was hoping for. You're a clever girl, my dear.'

'Thank you.' Sue smiled back with relief. 'I'm glad they're what you want. I must confess there are some pieces I'm rather fond of myself — that choker, for instance.'

'I like it too. It has a very oriental look.'

'It should do! I copied the design for the motif from one of Serena's Chinese carpets. I haven't the least idea what it means.'

'It's just a good luck symbol. Very appropriate!' Marsha tapped the paper with a long, scarlet finger-nail. 'I can imagine it adapted for earrings too, can't you? There was another design that interested me — ' She leafed through until she came to the one she was seeking. Sue became aware that the quality of her smile had changed. Strangely there seemed a certain sly triumph about it. 'I have to ask you,' she said. 'You are quite sure these are your own work?'

'Of course they are! I've been busy all week on them.' Sue was aware that her voice had risen indignantly and forced herself to calm down. 'I assure you they're original,' she added quietly.

'Excuse me a moment.' Marsha swiftly left

the room and was back a minute or two later, holding something out to Sue. 'You see why I asked,' she said. 'This is curiously like your design, isn't it?' She was still smiling, not too worried that she had apparently caught Sue out in a piece of mild plagiarism. She would be able to drive a harder bargain.

Sue looked in disbelief at the object she took from Marsha. It was the bracelet — *Mali*'s bracelet! But how could it be? How could it be here, now, when Mali was dead? Unless Marsha — unless Marsha — her thoughts whirled.

'What do you think of it?' Marsha's voice seemed to come from a long way off and Sue swallowed hard, trying to pull herself together sufficiently to answer her.

'Where on earth did you get this?' she managed to ask at last. 'It *is* one of my designs, no doubt about it. See, there's a little curled S inside? That's my trademark.'

'Well, isn't that incredible?' Marsha came and sat down beside her, all friendliness and warmth again. 'It was brought to me from Bangkok.'

'Small world,' Sue said, with a twitch of the lips that was supposed to be a smile. 'I suppose — I suppose whoever gave it to you must have bought it there. The design seemed to me just as suitable for Hong Kong as anywhere else — but if you'd rather delete it — '

'Not at all; it's charming.' Marsha took the bracelet back again and turned it between her fingers. 'Such a strange coincidence, though. I am surprised — I mean, the person who gave it to me was hardly likely to have paid much. It might even have been stolen, perhaps, and resold on a market-stall. As you say, the world is a small place.' She put the bracelet down on the table, dismissing it from her thoughts. 'I've managed to find a man who will do the actual production work — a real craftsman. I should like you to meet him. But first, perhaps, we should talk terms.'

As Bruno had surmised, Marsha drove a hard bargain. But Sue knew her own worth and was not too worried whether Marsha bought her work or not; she felt the designs were good enough for her to see when she got back to London where the eastern influence in fashion was strong. But eventually they sat back mutually pleased with the arrangements that had been made.

'I wish you were staying in Hong Kong,' Marsha said. 'I can see this growing into a profitable partnership for both of us. Have you thought of it?'

'Staying here? No, I haven't. Oh, it's a

fascinating place and I love it, but professionally London is the place where it's at.'

Marsha's smile grew arch and full of meaning. 'Perhaps a certain someone will make you change your mind, eh? Who knows what the future will hold? I know a certain tall, dark and handsome man who would very much like you to stay.'

Sue smiled back politely, refusing to be drawn, and gathering up her drawings she replaced them in the portfolio.

'Well,' Marsha said, getting briskly to her feet now that the interview was over. 'I'm sure we'll do very good business together, whatever the future. May I ring you in a few days to arrange a meeting with the man I mentioned?'

'Of course.' Sue stood up too. She had her back to the huge windows, but Marsha's view of the terrace was unobstructed and she could tell from the older woman's frown that Edward had once more come into view. She turned and, sure enough, his slight figure was approaching them from the direction of the pool. This time he could scarcely avoid acknowledging their presence, but a curt and unsmiling nod was as far as he would go.

'How very solitary he looks!' Sue remarked, almost to herself.

'I worry about him.' Marsha spoke

abruptly, as if such an admission was uncharacteristic.

'Perhaps he will find himself, once he gets to Oxford.'

'Find himself?' His mother raised her eyebrows. 'You are right, Sue. He seems lost. He says he doesn't belong in our world.'

'Surely teenagers, by definition, have to rebel against their parents. He'll grow out of it.'

'I hope you're right.' Marsha turned away from the window. 'He was always a solitary child and I have always been occupied with the business. Perhaps too much, I don't know.' She looked at her watch as if suddenly reminded of her pressing concerns. 'Heavens above, look at the time. I have an appointment in Kowloon in five minutes. Please forgive me if I rush off, won't you?'

'Of course.' She was relieved that the interview was at an end. She had deliberately put the incident of the bracelet out of her mind, forcing herself to concentrate on the business in hand just as she would have done if the bracelet had been of no significance, yet she was dying to have a moment on her own to think over the implications.

'How are you getting back home?' Marsha asked. 'Have you a car?'

'No I came by taxi.'

'Oh dear! I'd give you a lift, but I *am* so rushed — '

'Please, don't worry. If I could just use your phone, I'll call a cab.'

'Of course. Help yourself. You'll find it in the hall.' She was gathering up her bag, her car-keys, her briefcase, as she spoke and Sue followed her out into the hall.

'I'll be in touch,' Marsha said as she opened the heavy front door. 'Goodbye, my dear. Forgive me for being in such a hurry. The phone is over there.'

'Thank you.' Sue stood at the top of the steps and waved a hand as Marsha drove off at speed in her Alfetta, scattering the gravel on the drive and causing one of the gardeners who had been raking it with painstaking thoroughness to look after her in dumb resignation.

Sue went back into the house and dialled the number which by this time had become very familiar to her. A cab, she was assured, would be at the house in a few minutes.

Meanwhile she stood in the hall and looked around curiously. Another thick carpet, another chandelier, more lilies. And, permeating all, the sickly scent of the unseen joss-sticks.

The house was silent and appeared empty, yet she knew that somewhere Edward was there, behind one of those closed doors. Upstairs or down? She had no way of knowing, but as she looked upwards and admired the shallow sweep of the stairs that seemd to her perhaps the most beautiful feature of this heavily over-decorated house, she heard a sound. It was a typewriter, operated with great rapidity. Whoever was working up there was no two-finger typist, picking hesitantly over the keys, but someone to whom the use of a typewriter was common practice.

She listened intently. It meant nothing, she told herself; merely that Edward, in common with millions of others, could use a typewriter. Yet a sample of type would prove conclusively one way or the other if he had written the letters to Neil. In view of the fact that Marsha was in possession of the bracelet, it seemed even more likely that he might have done so. He could be in a position to know about the girls, if his parents were involved in the organisation.

She started for the stairs. They went straight up for a short distance, then curved to a galleried landing. The noise seemed to be coming from behind a door set in the centre of the landing and with her eyes on this, her hand trailing on the banister, she slowly ascended. She had no fixed plan in her mind.

She would have to play it off the cuff, she thought — perhaps she could prevail on Edward to offer her coffee and would have an opportunity to filch a page of typescript while he was ordering it. Perhaps there would be some discarded pages in the wastepaper-basket. The important thing was to get inside that room.

'Missee!' The harsh voice from below made her heart leap with shock and she turned to see a small woman standing several feet below her. She was dressed in the traditional clothes of an amah — black trousers and white, high-necked blouse. Her small, skeletal face was a network of lines and her wispy hair was scraped back in a tight knot. She seemed to have materialised from nowhere.

Sue held her hand to her heart and laughed down at her.

'Oh, you made me jump,' she said. 'I didn't hear you come.'

There was no answering smile on the Chinese woman's face and her black eyes smouldered with hostility.

'Where you go?' She almost spat the question at Sue.

'I was going to see Edward. He is up there, isn't he?'

'Master Edlard? No, no, NO!' Sue looked bewildered at the vehemence of her reply, particularly as she accompanied it by advancing towards her and grasping her elbow with a grip like iron. 'Master Edlard work. He want no visitor.'

'I wouldn't interrupt him for long.'

'He work. No visitor.'

'What *is* going on?' The door at the top was flung open and a cold-faced Edward appeared. The amah spoke to him in rapid Cantonese, still gripping Sue's arm like a policeman taking a felon into custody.

'You wanted to see me?' Edward asked her brusquely. 'I'm afraid I'm rather busy.'

'Do you think,' Sue said, suddenly furiously angry, 'you could ask this woman to take her hands off me? I was making a social call, not stealing the family silver.'

For the first time showing a glimmer of a smile, Edward spoke to the amah who let go Sue's arm and muttering under her breath moved off towards the kitchen quarters whence she had, presumably, emerged.

'I apologise for Ying,' Edward said. 'She is, perhaps, somewhat over-protective of my interests. I am, as I said, very busy. There's a lot to clear up before I leave next week.'

'Then I won't disturb you further.' Sue could see that her cause was lost before it had begun. There was obviously no way that Edward was going to let her into that room. 'I merely wanted to wish you well for your new life in England.'

'How kind!' There was no expression in Edward's voice. 'Er — I believe a taxi has just arrived. For you, perhaps?'

'For me. Thank you.' For what? she asked herself, as she went down the stairs, leaving Edward standing at the top of the staircase looking after her. Of all the ill-mannered, oafish young men she had ever had the bad luck to meet!

But he did own a typewriter and he could use it. Before she had reached the front door she had changed her mind about going back to the house on the Peak. She had to see Neil — and that might well be easier said than done. He had mentioned that he spent little time at the office of the 'Gazette', looking in only to pick up his mail and submit his copy. Most of the time he was either out and about after a story or working at home. Maybe, with a bit of luck, she would find him at the flat — at any rate she would take the risk and ask the taxi-driver to take her there.

She was in luck. Neil opened the door to her, looking dishevelled as if he had been disturbed in the middle of some highly concentrated piece of composition. Indeed his typewriter, now mute in the middle of a sea of papers on the table, gave the impression of smoking quietly, recovering from a furious bout of activity.

'I'm sorry to disturb you,' Sue said.

'Not a bit — it's nice to see you. Come on in.'

'There was something I had to tell you.'

'I've been meaning to ring you.' Neil gestured at the cluttered table. 'I've been up to my eyes this week, one way and another. Do sit down and tell me your news.'

'I've just come from the Wongs,' she said and told him about Marsha producing the bracelet.

'Did you let her know that there was only one in existence?'

'No, of course not. She thinks it was a run-of-the-mill production. And, what's more, Neil, Edward Wong uses a typewriter so he could have written the letters.'

'But *would* he? Even given the fact that he knows about his father's activities, would he really want to shop him? Somehow it doesn't seem feasible.'

'Perhaps not. But there was no doubt whatever about the bracelet.'

Neil was on his feet, unable in his eagerness to stay in one place. 'I knew it — I *knew* it,' he said, slapping his clenched fist into the palm of his other hand as he ranged around his tiny sitting-room. 'I knew that bloody man had to have a hand in it. No, that's not entirely fair, there are others just as bad, but I knew it was someone like that; someone powerful and power-mad. You heard him the other night at your brother's house. He doesn't give a damn for anyone other than himself. He'd be just the boy to persuade himself that even white slavery was justified because it made money.'

'Do you think Marsha is a party to it?'

'She must be, surely?'

'I don't know. I suppose she must. Neil, if only I could have pinched a sample of typescript!'

'Can't be helped.' He was staring at her unseeingly, thoughtfully chewing a knuckle. 'It might be a case for a little breaking and entering.'

'Oh no, surely not! You could get into terrible trouble.'

'Not me — I'd get a professional to do it. There are one or two crooks around this town who owe me a favour. The only snag is that there's no one on earth more security-conscious than your rich Chinese. I'm willing to bet they have dogs patrolling at night.'

'It all sounds a bit hopeless.'

'I've *got* to prove who wrote those letters — it's the key to the whole thing.'

'You haven't got anywhere since I last saw you?'

Neil pulled a face at her. 'No, you beat me there. I've been tackling the problem from the other end. A friend of mine in Bangkok has been trying to find the guardian woman you saw, but she seems to have disappeared without trace.' He ran his hands through his hair. 'I don't seem to have had a minute to concentrate on it this week. I've been doing the entertainments column on top of everything else. I haven't had a night off since I can't remember when.'

'Is that why you haven't phoned me?' The question came out almost involuntarily and Sue could feel herself blushing at the artlessness of it. Neil sat down and regarded her with a quirk of amusement.

'I rather thought your attention was more than fully engaged by friend Bruno.'

'How do you know that?'

He narrowed his eyes and adopted a heavy middle-European accent. 'My spies are everywhere.'

'I see. And what have they reported?'

Neil opened his mouth to speak, then shut it again. 'I was only kidding,' he said. 'I don't know anything about anything.'

Sue sighed. 'Oh boy, this is a small town.'

'That it is, my sweet. And in small towns

people gossip, especially about larger-than-life characters like Bruno with a string of conquests behind them.'

'To hell with everybody,' Sue said, suddenly feeling miserable. 'Let them think what they like.'

'Sure,' Neil readily agreed. 'To hell with them all. Would you like a beer?'

'Thank you, I would.' She was left looking bleakly into space while he went into the kitchen. Now why, she thought, do I feel this way — as if things have suddenly gone disastrously wrong? She had been seeing a lot of Bruno. Up to this moment the direction and extent of their relationship had seemed a problem for her alone. The thought that other people — Neil too? — had found it a subject for speculation shouldn't, surely, come as a surprise. Yet she felt absurdly upset that other people — especially Neil? — might have got the wrong idea. She got up and went into the kitchen.

'Neil, I'm not one of them.'

He threw her a glance as he poured the beer, amused and puzzled.

'One of whom?'

'Bruno's conquests. I — I just wanted to put the record straight. Not that it matters.'

'Of course not,' he agreed. 'Your life is your own.' But he grinned at her with sudden happiness, the air clear between them. 'Would you like a ham sandwich? It must be just about lunch-time surely?'

They carried the food and drinks back to the sitting-room, a much easier atmosphere lightening Sue's spirits.

'I was thinking,' Neil said, 'are you doing anything tomorrow?'

'No, I don't think so.' The question seemed to open up all sorts of possibilities and Sue looked at him with interest. 'Why?'

'Because I have just this minute decided I'm taking the day off. It's more than three weeks since I had one and if I work like the clappers for the rest of today I'll be up to date with my copy, so I'll fix it with the editor this afternoon. We'll have a day out.'

'Lovely! Doing what?'

'I have a friend,' Neil said, 'with a junk. Not a super-duper stream-lined craft like the Wongs have, but nevertheless a junk. It's a scruffy, sawn-off little thing but quite seaworthy — and, best of all, it's available. John's on leave in England and said I could borrow it any time. What do you say?'

'I think it sounds marvellous.'

'We'll leave all this sordid mess behind us for one day and forget everything. Would you like another sandwich?'

'No thanks, I've had plenty. Tomorrow I'll bring the food.'

'Great. I'll pick you up at ten o'clock — OK?'

'Fine. Where shall we go?'

Neil chewed in silence for a few moments, considering the possibilities.

'Let's play it by ear,' he said. 'See how we feel. We can go out towards the islands and anchor somewhere; have a swim over the side, explore a bit. It'll be fun.'

'Let's hope it keeps fine.'

Neil looked over towards the window, at the cloudless sky outside and the heat that seemed to shimmer tangibly, kept at bay only by the pulsating air-conditioner, and he laughed.

'How English can you get?' he asked. 'Never sure of the sun, even in a Hong Kong summer. It'll be beautiful, Sue. Just beautiful.'

★   ★   ★

'What did I tell you?'

They were waiting on the jetty for the little sampan to come and collect them and ferry them to the junk. It was already hot. The sun blazed from a sky in which small white clouds drifted lazily like puffs of smoke. All round them were moored boats of all kinds, from impressive yachts to half-submerged wrecks. There was a slight breeze which caused them to rock gently at their moorings and ruffled the surface of the inlet, so that the tops of the waves glinted in the sun. Because it was mid-week there was little activity. Boat-owners who would be disporting themselves at sea during the weekend were now busy at their office desks and only the fortunate few were at liberty to enjoy themselves.

Such peace, thought Sue. Peace and tranquillity and normality. The water slapped against the side of the jetty.

'I think I needed this rather badly,' she said.

Neil nodded. 'I know I did.'

Thickly wooded cliffs, clothed in deepest green, rose from the water's edge on the far side of the inlet — up, up to where a grey stone wall snaked round its contours, marking the position of the twisty road to Shek-O. So far above them that it looked like a toy, they could see a red, double-decker bus, its top storey just visible over the wall.

The sampan drew alongside the jetty and they loaded it with their things, exchanging pleasantries with the toothless, incredibly wrinkled old man who sat at the helm. He increased the revs and they chugged out into the middle of the inlet in the direction Neil indicated.

'Which is ours?' Sue asked.

Neil grinned at her. 'Don't jump the gun. Let it come as a surprise. Look, what do you think of that junk over there?'

He pointed to a magnificent teakwood vessel, its proud, uplifted rear deck polished and burnished and equipped with immaculate lounging furniture. A flurry of activity among the boat-boys seemed to indicate that it too was about to be taking a trip.

'That's the most beautiful thing I ever saw!'

'Guess who owns it.'

'Paul Wong?'

'You're telepathic. Don't let it give you ideas above your station. Ours isn't quite so beautiful, but she has one hell of a lot of character. Look, there she is.'

'Oh, no!' Sue burst out laughing. 'I don't believe it. Are you sure it's seaworthy?'

'Bet your life. Shh, stop laughing — you'll hurt her feelings.' Neil leapt aboard the junk as the sampan came alongside, and held out a hand to pull Sue on board after him. The boatman handed over their belongings.

Even Neil had to admit that it was not at all luxurious. The timbers badly needed a coat of paint, but they seemed in good repair and there was a reassuringly sturdy sound about the beat of its engine. They unlocked the cabin, which was neatly fitted with a tiny galley and a toilet compartment, and brought out the foam mattresses from the two bunks.

'We can use them for sunbathing later,' Neil said. He sniffed at them. 'They could do with an airing.'

'It all smells a bit damp down here,' Sue called from the cabin where she was stowing the food.

'It's bound to — but actually for a boat that hasn't been used for a couple of months it's incredibly dry. I'll get the bilge pumps going and we'll be right as rain.'

They nosed slowly past the other boats that were moored nearby, but once these were left behind Neil increased the speed and they were soon out in the middle of the inlet, chugging towards the open sea with a dignified roll. Sue climbed on top of the roof of the cabin which provided a conveniently flat sunbathing area and sat, hugging her knees, the wind streaming through her hair. She was dressed in a bikini underneath a brief pair of sky-blue shorts and her thin cotton blouse was knotted above her waist. She looked over her shoulder and smiled at Neil, behind and below her at the wheel.

'This is the life. Let's sail away, for a year and a day.'

'I'll be out of gas before then.'

'Don't be so prosaic.' She stretched her arms as if embracing the sea and the sky and the distant islands. 'This is the Hong Kong I love. You can keep the crowds.'

'Have you been to the New Territories yet?'

'Only to the golf club at Fanling.'

'Then you'll have seen the lovely rolling hills. I must take you there one day. One can walk and walk all day — it's as remote and unspoilt as rural China.'

'I'd like to go to the border.'

'Yes, I suppose one has to really, though there's nothing much to see.' He nodded out towards the horizon. 'See those islands way over there? The ones really far out? That's Red China. Go over there and you're good and clobbered. It's up with the gunboat and into jail.'

'Truly?'

'Truly, cross my heart. But have no fear. I've studied my charts and passed my exams.'

'A master-Marriner, in fact?'

'Don't think you're the first to make that crack!'

They were passing a tiny, conical-shaped island on their port bow, apparently uninhabited, and Sue looked at it curiously.

'What are all those stones on the side of the hill?' she asked.

'Graves,' Neil told her.

'People come all this way to be buried?' She swivelled round and looked at him in amazement. 'But there don't seem to be any live people here! Why should they bring dead ones such a long way?'

'Have you heard of fung shui? It's a sort of mystical combination of elements that makes a place favoured by the spirits and brings good luck. You have to watch the fung shui when you're building a house, or even positioning the furniture in a room, and it's especially important when you're buried.' He nodded towards the graves. 'The fung shui must be good here.'

'How would you find out whether it is or not?'

'You employ your friendly neighbourhood necromancer.' The answer in this strangely beautiful setting seemed eminently reasonable.

'Why didn't I think of that?' Sue threw back her head and laughed suddenly. 'Oh, I *do* like this place,' she said.

'Me too.'

'In spite of everything?'

' 'Everything' being corruption?'

'Yes. And Triads and vice-rings and overcrowding; and half Hong Kong being demolished to build bigger and better sky-scrapers and the other half being dug up to build the metro.'

'Talking of corruption,' Neil began, his voice suddenly sombre.

'But we're not. Not today — please Neil.'

'All right.' They chugged on for a while, Neil whistling to himself. Sue looked at him pensively over her shoulder. She sighed.

'OK,' she said at last. 'What were you going to say.'

Neil shrugged. 'Honestly, it's a bit pointless to say anything. You're right not to want to discuss it.'

'That's infuriating!'

'Sorry. It's just that I'm not entirely sure of my facts. It's only unsubstantiated gossip.'

'About whom?'

Neil hesitated. 'Bruno. He could be in trouble, Sue.'

Sue climbed down from the cabin roof and came to stand beside him.

'Why? What's he done?'

'He's said to have done some large-scale fiddling with quotas.'

'I don't understand.'

'Well, in the rag-trade there's this thing called the quota system. Firms are only allowed to export so much — it's a sort of protection for the E.E.C. countries — and naturally this can cause a bit of heart-burning with the larger manufacturers, who want to export a greater quantity. Some firms, on the other hand, may have difficulty in filling their quota. My information is that Bruno has been acting as a sort of quota-broker, if you like — and naturally taking a very hefty rake-off along the way.'

'How do you know all this?'

'The I.C.A.C. have been investigating some chap he's very closely associated with. I gather it's only a matter of time before they get around to Bruno.'

'What would happen to him?'

'I don't know. I don't know the extent of his involvement or what sort of money we're talking about. If he's been taking bribes to any large extent, he could be in dead trouble. Look — this is a nice bay. Shall we anchor here?'

Sue looked about her vaguely, her mind far away. Blast Bruno — she thought she was getting away from him, just for one day. It was as if he had reached out and dimmed a little of the brightness that had enclosed them. 'Yes,' she said at last. 'Yes, this looks fine.'

Neil killed the engine and busied himself with the anchor.

'Do you feel like a swim? That beach looks rather inviting.'

'Yes.' At her listless agreement Neil looked at her and, seeing her troubled expression, came close and took her by the shoulders, shaking her gently.

'Come on, Sue. He'll probably wriggle out of it, just like he's wriggled out of everything else. Don't let him spoil our day.'

'No, damn it! I'm not going to let him do that.' She unzipped her shorts and peeled off her blouse, revealing a white bikini underneath them, went to the head of the ladder and dived off into the blue water of the bay. She swam away from the boat with a measured and purposeful crawl, and Neil watched for a moment with tightened lips. She had *said* she didn't care about Bruno, hadn't she? But he should have had more sense than to tell her. He was one of the family, after all. He sighed, stepped out of his jeans and joined her in the water.

He caught her up easily. She had turned over on her back and was floating, looking up at the sky. He trod water beside her.

'Don't be cross,' he said.

'I'm not. In fact I'm greatly obliged to you for telling me.'

'Let's swim to the beach.'

'I'll race you.' Sue flipped quickly over and darted away.

By the time they reached the small, curved

beach the shadow that had fallen over the day seemed to have lifted a little. There was a physical feeling of well-being that insisted on edging out the depression and, when Neil held out his hand to her to help her up the steeply shelving beach, she smiled at him.

'It was just that, momentarily, I'd forgotten all sorts of ugly things were going on back there,' she said, as if continuing a conversation.

'I know. Let's walk.'

Still with her hand in his, they went along the beach, bending now and then to look in a pool or pick up a shell.

'Such luxury,' Neil said. 'To be so solitary.'

'One forgets what it's like.'

'You know who I feel sorry for? The young lovers. They have no seclusion, no little space for themselves. Just crowded homes and crowded streets — beaches packed with people, and nice little picnic-places, all swarming with their fellow men.'

'There's this.' Sue waved her free hand all about her.

'For this, you need a boat. And for a boat you need money.'

'Yes, of course. Sometimes I'm a bit unimaginative about things like that.'

'Never having wanted for anything your-self?'

'Something like that. Nothing material, anyway.'

Neil lowered himself to the sand and pulled her down beside him.

'Tell me all,' he commanded. 'What did you *not* have?'

'Brothers and sisters. Oh, I had Ian, of course, and he was always marvellous to me, but he was grown up, it seemed to me, before I was born. I used to long for a sister to play with.'

'There's never a happy medium, is there? I had two brothers and three sisters and many a time I wished them further. Pesky creatures, they were, those sisters of mine.'

'But you must have had fun. Do tell me about them.'

All the shadows were gone now. Communication between them was easy — a matter of elliptical phrases and half-finished sentences. Sometimes there were silences. Sue looked at him after a particularly protracted one and he seemed to be asleep — at any rate his eyes were shut, his thick, tawny lashes lowered like little fans. She took advantage of the moment to study the finely marked brows and high cheek-bones, the rather large, slightly curved nose, the sensitive mouth. She looked away when he opened his eyes, suddenly shy.

'Let's get back to the junk,' he said, sitting up, 'before we perish from malnutrition. I'm starved, I don't know about you.' He got to his feet and reached down to give her a helping hand.

They stood for a moment, only inches apart, facing each other. Slowly his hands travelled up her arms and came to rest on her shoulders. Bending, he kissed her on the lips, then held her slightly away from him, his eyes and mouth smiling as his gaze moved over her face.

'You know something?' he asked. 'You're the loveliest thing.'

The kiss this time was a more mutual affair.

'Maybe we should go and have lunch,' he said, without moving when they eventually drew away.

'I'm sure you're right.' Sue's voice emerged as a shaky whisper. But they stayed where they were and kissed again.

At last they moved off down the beach, arms round each other, not speaking. They looked at each other from time to time and smiled, their thoughts, had they known it, strangely similar. Was this, they were asking themselves, as different as it seemed? They had both been kissed before, both fancied themselves in love, both felt themselves committed to other people in the past. Could this really be something more? Could this be — could this be —

Sue's thoughts sheered away. Just enjoy it, she told herself. He's here and you're here — don't look beyond the moment. Time will prove all things, one way or the other.

They swam back to the boat and hauled themselves up the ladder. Lunch was crusty rolls and Stilton, Poully Fuissé and peaches, and it seemed like a banquet. Afterwards they dragged the foam cushions into the shade.

Neil, lying beside her, leant over and kissed her lingeringly.

'Just hark to that resounding silence,' he said at last. 'Me, the great spinner of words. Somehow I can't think of a single thing to say that hasn't been said a million times before. Which would you prefer? 'Shall I compare thee to a summer's day?' Or 'This could be the Start of Something Big?' Either is equally appropriate.'

'Thank you — I'll take Shakespeare.'

'Mm, he's yours. You have the loveliest ears, did you know that? I shall probably write a sonnet to them.'

Sue laughed. 'Somehow I don't imagine you could stretch my ears to fourteen lines of iambic pentameter.'

'You will come out to dinner with me

tonight, won't you? Somewhere grand and glorious and fabulously expensive.'

'Oh Neil, I can't.' She reached out and traced the line of his eyebrows. 'I wish I could, but we're booked to go to some terribly formal dinner-party. It's not the sort of free-for-all where I won't be missed — the animals will go in two by two. Ian and Serena are going.'

'And you're paired off with Bruno?'

Sue nodded. 'Yes, but for the last time. It's a state of affairs that's got to stop.'

'I'll second that.'

'Neil, should I give him any sort of warning about — about what you told me?'

'I rather think it's all too late. My instinct is to say, stay out of it. I'd give a lot not to have told you — journalists should be more discreet.'

'Perhaps.' She twined his thick, unruly hair in her fingers and pulled him down to her, feeling his lips on her throat, on her shoulders. She closed her eyes because suddenly the happiness seemed almost too much to be borne.

Sex is the strangest thing, she thought. Her relationship with Steve, which she had called love, had been turmoil from the start. There had been no peace, no confidence. Excitement, yes — plenty of that, in the beginning;

but how quickly it had turned to misery!

With Neil it all seemed as natural as breathing, this closeness. Just as if she had known him for ever.

★   ★   ★

The sun moved round and lay in a solid bar across Sue's exposed midriff.

'You mustn't get burnt,' Neil said.

'Maybe I should cover myself.' She made no effort to move.

'You'll be sorry if you don't.'

'Mm,' she assented lazily, her eyes closed. 'It'll all end in tears.'

Neil sat up and stretched. 'I'll get your blouse,' he said. He stood up, but stopped in his tracks on his way to the cabin.

'Well, just look at that,' he said softly. 'We have company.'

Sue sat up and turned to follow his gaze, frowning. She was in no mood to share this particular paradise with anyone.

'Go away,' she urged under her breath, looking towards the magnificent junk that was moored at the other end of the bay.

'It's the Wongs'.' Neil went to the rail and leant over. 'Remember, we saw it when we were on our way out?'

'Yes, of course. Can you see who's on it?'

'It looks strangely deserted — no wait, there's someone on the side deck, I think. Pass me those binoculars, will you?'

He reached out a hand blindly, his eyes still fixed on the junk, and Sue put the glasses into his hand. He raised them to his eyes and grinned.

'What do you know,' he said. 'Looks like Edward has a little red blood in him after all. He has a girl with him.'

'Leave them alone, Neil.' Sue tugged at his arm. 'Don't be such a peeping Tom. How would you like it?'

'They're only talking.' But he did lower the binoculars, to stand with his brow furrowed in thought.

'What's wrong?' Sue asked him.

'That girl. I've seen her before somewhere, but damned if I can remember where.' He raised the glasses again.

'Is she dark-haired? Slight build? Rather slitty eyes, with a sallow complexion?' Sue put her arm through his and leaned her head against his shoulder. 'Ten to one she's Chinese.'

'Very amusing,' Neil said, taking a moment to aim a cuff at her, but continuing to watch. 'Wait, I've got it. I've *got* it.' The binoculars fell on their strap as he turned and grabbed Sue excitedly by the shoulders. 'I know where

I saw that girl last. It was when Chairman Mao died, years ago. There were big demonstrations here — memorial rallies, orations, queues of people in Statue Square waiting to sign their names in a book of condolence. I went down there to see if I could pick up the odd story or three and I spoke to this girl. She was clutching her little red book of Thoughts, tears streaming down her face. It was very moving.'

'So she's a communist.'

'A very militant one, I imagine. That's no crime, of course. Hong Kong is full of them — but do you see the significance? If she and Edward Wong are so friendly, it's a sure bet he's a communist too. And if he's a real one, as opposed to a teenager with vague leftish objections to his father's way of making money, it makes sense after all that he should denounce his parents' activities. The Party comes first. He wouldn't let a small thing like family loyalty stand in the way after all.'

'Well, I'm not surprised he's a communist,' Sue agreed. 'He sounded like one at the party, didn't he? Remember his remarks about both of you being wrong? About there being only one way to run the country? And before that, when I was talking to him, he made some very bitter remarks about the

121

upper classes, as if he were counting the days to the revolution.'

'I'm convinced, now, that he wrote those letters, Sue. I always thought he was capable of it — but it was the fact that his parents were involved that stuck in my throat. The Chinese have a great feeling for family and it just didn't seem to make sense that he'd want his own parents investigated, whatever they'd done. But this explains everything.'

'So what will you do?'

'Pay him a visit tomorrow.' He sighed and held Sue close to him. 'I don't want this day to end, do you?'

'We can have other days, can't we?'

'That we can. I feel a little sorry that we didn't go very far today — '

'We went quite far enough.'

Laughing, Neil bent to kiss her. 'You know what I mean. Mile-wise. Let's plan to go to Cheung Chau next time. It's a lovely little island and I want you to see it.'

'When will that be?'

Neil considered. 'Why not Saturday? I'm so up to date with my work it's unbelievable. It's something I'd like to make the most of.'

'Saturday's fine with me. Oh, that's only the day after tomorrow — how lovely!'

'I guess I might survive till then.'

'Look.' Sue nodded towards the other,

grander junk. 'They're leaving.'

'And so ought we, I suppose. Come on, now — you can learn to make yourself useful. Up with that anchor, girl.'

'Aye aye, sir. You're the master Mariner.' Laughing, they fell into each other's arms.

★ ★ ★

'Good day?' Serena asked dutifully, not taking her eyes from the television screen. She was curled up in an armchair in the sitting-room and Sue collapsed into its twin, not in the least interested in the soap opera that was emoting away in front of them but too worn out by the sun and fresh air to go a step further. Neil had dropped her at the house, refusing to come in. She would need to get ready for the evening ahead, he had said, and he had work to do. I wonder if that was all? Sue wondered. Was he, perhaps, a little afraid that he might meet Bruno?

'Oh, it was a lovely day,' she said now, leaning back into the depths of the armchair. 'Ian not in yet?'

Serena shook her head wordlessly and Sue closed her eyes, smiling. It was quite impossible to talk to her sister-in-law while she was engrossed in this endless serial, but she was happy to wait. The beautifully dim, uncluttered room was blissfully restful after the heat outside.

The credit titles eventually rolled and Serena uncoiled herself sufficiently to lean over and press the remote-control button that switched the set off.

'That thing is nothing but a con,' she said. 'I've been waiting all week to find out what Snapper said to Sally and whether Chris found out about the baby, and have they told us? No they haven't! They've fobbed us off with that dim sister of his and that ghastly Mrs Chancellor.'

'That's what it's all about, isn't it?' Lazily Sue tilted her head round to look at Serena. 'They spin out the agony, just so they can say 'Continued in our Next!' '

'I'm going to give it up.' Serena spoke with determination, as if she were forswearing smoking or drugs.

'I'll believe that when I see it. Sometimes I think that those people are more real to you than those of us you see every day.'

'Sue, that's an awful thing to say!' Serena sat up straight and looked horrified.

'I was only kidding.' But was she, Sue asked herself? There was no doubt that Serena had seemed very remote lately and there had not been the same rapport between them since Bruno had come back to Hong

Kong. Maybe she was wearing out her welcome. Maybe she should soon think of leaving.

'Serena, you will say if I'm getting on your nerves, won't you? If you want me to go?'

'You're no trouble, Sue. Stay as long as you like.'

'Thank you. Something's eating you though, isn't it?'

Serena sighed. 'Not really. Well, not much.'

'What is it?'

Serena hesitated. 'Suddenly my past seems to be catching up with me,' she said at last. 'I'm not particularly proud of the way I behaved before I met Ian, but I didn't brood about it until recently. I felt I'd put it all behind me. But now Bruno keeps reminding me. Then today you go out with Neil Marriner.'

'What's that got to do with it?'

'He knows all about me. He must have told you.'

'He hasn't said a word, except that you were the belle of Hong Kong. Stop seeing ghosts, Serena. It's what you are now that counts. Ian adores you! Who else matters?'

'Suppose he should stop?'

'He won't. He's a bit late tonight, isn't he?'

'There's some sort of flap on. Evidently the Banstead Marvell top man in Australia has absconded with the takings, or something — anyway, there's a very top man from Head Office out today, on his way to Sydney. Why he has to stop over in Hong Kong I have no idea, unless it's because no one from Head Office can move anywhere without causing the maximum amount of inconvenience to the greatest number of people. At least I haven't had to put him up. He's staying at the Mandarin.'

'When is he leaving?'

'Tomorrow night. Very late, of course, so that Ian has to drive him out to the airport at dead of night — and before that he wants to throw a cocktail party at his hotel. You'll come, won't you? As I recall from his last trip, he's partial to a pretty face.'

'Can Neil come too?'

'He's not very pretty.'

'Maybe not, but he's awful cute. Serena, I do want you two to be friends. He really is the greatest.'

Serena made a noise that was a kind of dubious sigh and got to her feet. 'I'm going to have a shower,' she said. 'I wish we didn't have to go out tonight.'

Sue laughed. 'Doesn't it strike gloom into your heart to think that Mrs — Mrs Sanderson, is it? — is probably groaning at this very moment and wishing that she could have a quiet night with her feet up, instead of all of us coming to dinner? Why don't we do everyone a favour and cancel the whole thing? Say we've all gone down with bubonic plague, or something. Just a mild dose, of course. What is the point of it all, Serena?'

Serena drew a deep breath and straightened her shoulders.

'It makes the wheels of commerce go round in a pleasant, civilised manner,' she said primly and left the room full of righteousness.

Sue laughed. Whatever the secrets of Serena's murky past, she had certainly joined the ranks of the respectable now. Maybe, she thought vaguely, it was like Catholics. Everyone said that a convert to the cause was stronger in his belief than one born in the faith. By that token, Serena must have been quite a swinger. But what did it matter now? Bruno was being all kinds of a bastard to keep reminding her of it.

She grimaced as she thought of Bruno. She hadn't mentioned to Serena the news that Neil had told her, as there seemed no sense in worrying everyone over something that might not be solid fact. Perhaps there might be a chance to give him an oblique hint tonight. What was almost more pressing, in her mind, was the need to let him know once and for all that she was not interested in going out with him again. If only she'd had the sense to recognise him for the predator he was, that first day when he had put in his surprise appearance by the pool.

Petulantly she frowned and thumped the arm of the chair with her clenched fist. Damn Bruno! He and all his works were an unwelcome intrusion, just now when she wanted to concentrate on being happy.

Oh, it had been a lovely, lovely day! And something warned her that the evening would be an equally sure-fire disaster.

6

Bruno was humming to himself as he poured the drinks. Life was certainly full of surprises. He had been just about ready to give up on Sue, until she had given him the unmistakable come-on after dinner. The men had finished sitting over the inferior port and it had been a relief to join the ladies, even though the conversation had continued on the incredibly boring level it had sustained all evening.

She was quite a girl, no doubt about it. That Nordic kind of beauty really turned him on — well, let's face it, he thought, the oriental kind did too, but Sue would be outstanding in any company. He couldn't remember when any bird had held out so long; he would, he thought, be able to prove the old adage that the harder they came, the harder they fell, and it was with a pleasant sense of anticipation that he turned round towards Sue and carried the drinks over to her, a smile on his handsome face.

Sue watched him cautiously. There was a whole carillon of warning bells ringing in her head. Far from the submissive and compliant girl of his hopes, she had been cursing herself for agreeing to his proposal that they should go back to his flat after the dinner-party, ever since her first initial assent to the idea. A few moment's thought should have told her that, although she wanted an opportunity to talk to him, to do it this way was asking for trouble.

The dinner-party had been a bore of the first magnitude, with excessive attention paid to protocol and none at all to the quality of the conversation or the harmonious mixture of guests. The men lingered over their port to the point where Sue felt that she would probably be spending the rest of her life listening to the other women discussing their servant problems. She had caught Serena's eye on one occasion at the exact point in time when they were both struggling to suppress a yawn and they both had to look away and bite their lips to keep from laughing.

There had been no opportunity to have a word with Bruno and his whispered suggestion that she should go back with him to the flat for a night-cap seemed, for one brief second, to provide the answer. It was only when she saw the hot, anticipatory gleam in his eye that she had misgivings and cursed herself for a fool. Of course he would think she was ripe for the killing, and who could blame him? She was old enough to know the score.

Perhaps, she had thought immediately, she could disillusion him on the journey. But fate was against this too, as just as they were about to drive away their hostess for the evening had stuck her head through the window. She had so many teeth that she gave the impression entering denture-first and Bruno recoiled as if bitten.

'Tell me,' she said. 'I *am* right, aren't I? You *do* live in Tai Tam Road? *Might* I ask you to do me the most enormous favour?'

Bruno smiled weakly and gestured in a 'be my guest' sort of way.

'It's a woman I have to help me on occasions like this. She lives quite near you — I wonder, would you be so kind? It's such an *awkward* journey at this time of night for the poor dear. Charles always has to take her, or else we have to try for a taxi.'

There seemed no way out of it. The woman was summoned and smiling broadly clambered into the back encumbered with several plastic bags which, judging from their aroma, contained left-overs from the lately consumed dinner. Barely concealing his annoyance, Bruno drove off amid effusive thanks from Mrs Sanderson and a gabble of incomprehensible English from the back seat.

Any confidences were obviously out of the question and Sue kept silent. So now the moment of truth had arrived.

The room was furnished in a lavish, aggressively modern way, with dark, upholstered units forming three sides of a square. A swift appraising glance had revealed that no single chair was within reach and she sat down in a corner waiting, with as much equanimity as she could muster, for the confrontation that inevitably had to come when Bruno sat down beside her. He put the two glasses down on the square tiled table in front of them and with the expertise of long practice managed to do so at the same time as he slid in beside her, putting his hand at the back of her head and pulling her towards him for a kiss that, wildly, she thought was going on for ever.

Eventually he seemed to become aware that she was not exactly responding with passion, but rather that she was trying to break away from him.

'Something wrong?' His dark eyes were puzzled.

'I've got to talk to you, Bruno.'

'After,' he said, reaching for her again. 'Afterwards, baby. We'll talk as much as you like.'

'Now,' she said, pushing him away and

escaping from his arms that now seemed as numerous as the tentacles of an octopus. He followed her into the middle of the room.

'Sweet Sue,' he breathed hoarsely. 'What's got into you? Don't you know how I want you?'

She slipped away from him again. 'Bruno, will you stop this and listen to me?' she said from the other side of the room. 'You're making both of us look ridiculous and I won't put up with it. Now stay right there, do you hear?'

He looked at her for a moment, the lustful light dying from his face, his expression becoming cold and watchful. 'Anything you say,' he said, reaching for a cigarette. 'It's no very big deal, after all.'

'Of course not,' Sue readily agreed. 'Why bother with me, when you have any number of girls ready to fall at your feet?'

'More to the point, why are you bothering with me?'

'I came for two reasons,' Sue said. 'If you sit down like a civilised human being I'll tell you. The first reason was to tell you — though I hardly think this is necessary after tonight — that going about together the way we've been doing has got to stop. I know as well as you that it's time I got burnt or came out of the kitchen, and I want out,

Bruno. I want to be friends, that's all.'

Bruno lifted his eyes to heaven. 'Heaven save us from that routine,' he said piously.

'Well, all right. Still, it was in friendship that I wanted to tell you about something else. Neil Marriner says that he thinks you could be in trouble with the I.C.A.C. I wanted to warn you, just in case you were in time to cover your tracks.'

Bruno exhaled slowly. 'Don't worry about me, baby. I've got friends in high places, which is more than one can say for Neil Marriner. He'll find himself out on his ear if he doesn't stop being so strident about the poor, underprivileged workers. When did he tell you all this, just as a matter of interest?'

'Today. We went out in a junk.'

Bruno looked at her expressionlessly. 'I thought there was something! I'll bet that it wasn't all sandwiches and sandcastles today, was it? Have you and Marriner got something going?'

'I think so. I think I could even be in love with him.'

Bruno threw back his head and laughed. 'You poor idiot! Don't you realise you'll always come second to the hungry masses? He's too debilitated by his bleeding heart to be much use to any girl.'

'On that note,' Sue said angrily, picking up

her handbag, 'I think I'll leave. Would you be kind enough to take me home, or shall I ring for a taxi?'

'Wait a minute!' Bruno was smiling again. 'Look, I'm sorry, Sue. Come on, sit down and finish your drink and then I'll take you home. Marriner's never been my cup of tea, you know that — you can hardly expect me to change my opinion now. When are you seeing him again?'

'Maybe tomorrow night at the Banstead Marvell cocktail party, if he can get away — or if not, we're going to Cheung Chau on Saturday. Why?'

'Because you can tell him from me that Wong hates his guts and that he's the one in trouble. I can look after myself.'

'I hope so. What's Wong likely to do to Neil?'

Bruno shrugged. 'No idea. He's just a nasty man to fall foul of.'

'I think Neil is aware of that. Bruno, please take me home now.'

'Sure.' They both stood up and made for the door, but before Sue had reached it she felt Bruno's hand on her shoulder. He swung her round to face him and pulled her close.

'I still don't see why it has to be this way,' he said, his lips caressing her temple. 'You drive me wild, Sue. I don't believe the attraction is only one-way.'

'Bruno, *please*!' She shoved him away. 'Just take me home, that's all I want.' She left him standing as she went outside and sat in the car.

A second later he joined her, his face tight with anger. Not a word passed between them on the way to the Peak. It was the end, Sue thought ruefully, of a not very beautiful friendship. All in all, it had been quite a day. Thank heaven for Neil! She stared out at the night as Bruno, his foot well down on the accelerator, swooped round the curves of the road to the Peak, wrenching the wheel as if it alone were the cause of his anger. If he expected her to show fear, he was disappointed. Her thoughts were much too far away.

7

Edward Wong, product of an English public school and destined for Balliol with all its ancient traditions, lay in a long, towelling-covered, foam-cushioned lounging-chair by the pool. Even if there had been anyone to see, his expression was hidden behind dark glasses. He was alone with his thoughts — and good, obedient, communist thoughts they were. He utterly despised the sybaritic luxury of his home, he told himself as he reached for his glass of chilled orange juice — and even more did he despise the methods by which his father had acquired the wherewithal to supply such luxury. He longed for the day when the red sun of China would fly over Hong Kong. Then, and only then, would decadent, swinish capitalists such as his father get their just deserts. Vacillating do-gooders like Neil Marriner, all words and no deeds, would be made to realise the true and glorious rewards that the new régime would bring.

He could hardly remember when he had first come under the spell of communist ideology. His parents had always seemed alien to him, perhaps because he saw them so seldom — they were always too busy making money to take much notice of what he was doing or thinking. It was Ying, his amah, who had moulded his character, and she, he realised now though he had been unaware of it at the time, who had fed him on the truths of communism and had fostered a hatred for his parents' way of life.

He had been miserable when the time had come to go away to England to school, but Ying had known how to console him. You must learn all you can, she told him, to be of maximum use when you are older. And it was Ying who had introduced him to the kindly man who had told him about communism and the rôle that he, Edward, could play once he was grown up. He had reinforced Ying's advice. Learn how to think like a Westerner, he had said. Learn, learn, learn. Learn how to talk like the upper-class, privileged member of society your parents want you to become. Then you will be of use when you are older.

He had understood little at that time, but he had been excited at the thought of becoming part of a mysteriously élite group of people. It was like a secret society for adults in which he was allowed to share. Since then, he thought, he had more than justified the faith they had placed in him. He had studied and read until, in all modesty, he considered he knew more about communism and the great Republic of China than any of them.

He now knew that they had plans for him. After he had graduated, which he intended to do with the greatest distinction possible, he was to apply for a job with the Colonial Government in Hong Kong. They would welcome him with open arms. Their policy was to employ educated Chinese these days and he would ensure that there would be none better educated than he. To Edward, on the threshold of his university career, life promised to be very interesting.

He was disturbed from his reverie by Ying, who gabbled at him in Cantonese about an English visitor who was waiting for him. He told her irritably to send him away, but before the words were out of his mouth he was annoyed to see the tall figure of Neil Marriner coming down the steps which led from the house to the pool area.

He raised his skinny figure and glared at the intruder.

'I don't think I remember asking you to come here,' he said coldly.

'You're right,' Neil agreed pleasantly, drawing up a chair close to Edward. 'But I knew you'd want to see me. I really think it's time we had a talk, don't you?' He turned to the amah and spoke to her in Cantonese. 'Thank you,' he said. 'You may go. The young master is pleased to see me.'

Edward spluttered indignantly. 'How dare you give orders to my servants?' But he waved the woman away nevertheless and she pattered away, a short-legged, diminutive figure in her baggy black trousers and white tunic. Neil watched her go.

'I'm sorry for bursting in like this,' he began. 'But I do feel we must get to the bottom of the affair you wrote about in your letters.'

Edward lay back and closed his eyes.

'I really haven't the first idea what you're talking about,' he said loftily. 'If you can't talk sense, I shall have to ask you to leave.'

Neil sighed. 'Don't let's waste time,' he said. 'I really am a very busy man. You know and I know that your parents are engaged in a very ugly business — business that concerns those girls you wrote about, the ones that have disappeared recently. For reasons best known to yourself, you chose to write to me anonymously — and you then followed this up with some high-flown invective, signifying your displeasure. What do you want of me, Edward? I can't publish hints and innuendos. I hate the idea of white slavery every bit as much as you do, but I need solid facts — and if you have any it's your duty to let me have them.'

'It's perfectly true that I despise my parents' activities,' Edward said. Neil waited, but he did not continue.

'It's also true that you're a communist, isn't it?'

Edward's head turned sharply to look at him. I wish his eyes weren't hidden, Neil thought. The inscrutable bloody Chinese don't need that sort of help.

'What gives you that idea?' Edward asked.

Strange, thought Neil. He sounds almost frightened. Now why should that be? It's no crime, as Sue said last night.

'For heaven's sake, you make it plain enough. If it's supposed to be a secret, you shouldn't go shooting your mouth off the way you do. Still less associate openly with a communist girl.'

'She happens to be a friend of mine.'

'I don't doubt it. She's a pretty girl. Maybe she talked you into sending the letter — '

'She knew nothing about it!' Edward said quickly and blushed scarlet.

'So you sent it all by yourself? Interesting! Just a personal distaste for this business, was it? I understand your feelings. Prostitution may be the oldest profession, but forcing young girls into it against their will seems about the most despicable thing I can think of.'

Edward was biting the inside of his lip in an agony of indecision. No longer was he the poised, arrogant young man Neil had known up to this point. His youth and immaturity were now apparent.

'Tell me about it,' Neil said, his voice gentle but authoritative.

'I — I found out about it by accident,' he said at last, so quietly that Neil had to strain to hear the words. 'We have quite a big library up at the house. I was in it one day, getting books from a bottom shelf. I heard my father come in with Kee — a man who works for him. I dislike him very much, so I kept very quiet. I didn't want to be bothered to talk to them and I thought they would soon go away. I was hidden, you see, behind a settee. It seemed best just to stay there.'

'Go on.'

'They started talking about the arrival of a girl from Bangkok, how she was to be taken to the second immigration desk at the airport. The immigration officer had been given his squeeze, Kee said.'

Neil nodded. 'What happened then?'

'They talked about taking the girl to the house in Deepwater Bay. I knew enough about my father's interests to know it must be a vice-ring,' the boy said, 'but I didn't know, then, the full extent of it. I found out soon enough, though. I'm often here alone and I went through his papers. There's a wall-safe behind a picture in the library. He doesn't know that I know the combination, but I worked it out years ago. It was a simple matter of mathematics and I'm rather good at mathematics. Anyway, I found the deeds of the house there and all the accounts. It made pretty horrific reading. There was a regular sum entered for bribes. I suppose they had to pay off the police as well as the immigration people.

'Yes, no doubt they did. So you decided to write to me?'

Edward's tongue flickered over his lips.

'Not then,' he said. 'I didn't know quite what to do. They are my parents, after all. But when I came home this July it seemed that they were determined to make my life a misery. I'd been used to freedom — they never cared where I went, or who I saw. But now, suddenly, I'm grown up. My mother insists I should accompany them everywhere, all in the name of education. They've dragged me around with them to their stupid, bourgeois dinner-parties and cocktail-parties until I felt like leaving home altogether. I was very angry after a particularly boring party and on impulse I wrote to you.'

Neil leant his head against the cushioned back-rest and gazed at the blue sky above him, his lips pursed into a soundless whistle. Now I've heard everything, he thought. It wasn't his great love for suffering humanity. It was just one cocktail-party too many.

'Your friends in the party must have been pleased with you,' he remarked lightly.

Edward turned to him, his face agitated. 'It has nothing to do with them. I'm — I'm supposed to keep quiet, not to draw attention to myself. That's why I wrote the way I did, without signing my name, just hinting. I thought you would do the rest. They would be angry if they found out about it, I think.' He swallowed hard. 'In fact, I *know* they would be angry.'

'Why would they?' Neil's voice was quietly neutral.

'I've told you, I'm not supposed to draw attention to myself.'

'They have plans for your future, is that right?'

Edward said nothing.

'I wonder if you know what you're getting yourself into,' Neil murmured.

'You don't have to worry about me.'

'I wonder. You know a girl died, don't you?'

Neil deliberately went off on this tack without warning and was rewarded by Edward's turning towards him again.

'No,' he said. 'I didn't know that.'

'Well, she did. Suicide is the official verdict. Found drowned in the harbour. But she was one of your father's girls all right and personally I think there might have been a lot more to it than that. What does your conscience say now?'

Only the continued biting of the inside of his cheek betrayed Edward's agitation.

'I know nothing about that,' he said.

'Have you ever seen the inside of this house?'

'No. They've never mentioned it to me, but I know where it is. It's a big house, hidden by a high wall, overlooking the bay.'

'I want the full address, Edward.' Neil's voice was suddenly forceful. 'More — I want the deeds you mentioned and the account books.'

The boy shook his head rapidly. 'Oh no,' he said. 'No, I can't give them to you. I told you, I mustn't be involved. I *won't* be involved. I refuse, absolutely.'

'You're afraid of the Party?'

'I'm not *afraid* of anyone,' he said, with a touch of his old arrogance. 'But the Party would be displeased, yes.'

'They need you sans peur and sans reproche until they give the word, is that right? For one who is supposed to keep his communistic leanings a secret, my lad, it appears to me that you have one hell of a lot to learn! One doesn't need to be exactly clairvoyant to know where your sympathies lie, you know.'

'Perhaps not.'

'You go shooting off your mouth at parties. You behave like a revolutionary straining at the leash. You'll be no use to them if you betray yourself like that.'

Edward took his glasses off at last and glared at Neil.

'You've said enough. I think you'd better leave.'

'I haven't quite finished. I want to put it to you this way, Edward. Either you give me the various documents I've asked for, or I will make it my business to talk to the editors of all the communist newspapers in Hong Kong. Believe it or not, I'm on quite friendly terms with some of them. I'll tell them about the letter you wrote me — even show it to them — and add the interesting titbit that you've told me what the Party has lined up for you in years to come.'

'But I haven't told you anything!'

'You don't need to. It's obvious they are

146

encouraging you to get a good, traditional Western education so that you can think in the Western way and operate at the highest government level once you leave university. I shall make it clear that you have, as they say in all the best spy stories, blown your cover to the non-communist press.'

'They'd never dare print it!'

'They wouldn't need to. The Party bosses would soon hear about it, wouldn't they — and that's all I'm interested in. Your future career as a communist agent would be finished before it began. They'd have no use for you after that.'

'That's blackmail!'

'If you like.' Silence lengthened between them.

'I can't win, can I?' Edward said bitterly. 'If I get the papers for you and my parents are arrested, it's bound to come out that I supplied the evidence. Attention will be drawn to me, which is just what they don't want.'

'I don't see why anyone should know your part in it. When do you leave for university?'

'Monday evening.'

'Well, there you are. Give me the papers during the day on Monday, as late as you like, and you'll be well away from here by the time the storm breaks.'

'Do I have your word on that?'

'My solemn promise.'

Edward thought it over some more and laughed bitterly.

'What a start to make in Oxford!' he said. 'Imagine what the Daily Mirror will make of it.'

'Oxford isn't what it was,' Neil pointed out. 'Maybe it will give you a certain cachet.'

'What will they get — my parents, I mean?'

'I don't know. No doubt they'll retain the best lawyer money can buy.'

'No doubt.'

'So where do we meet? And when?'

Edward thought about it. 'Say, five-thirty,' he said at last.

'OK. Where?'

'Somewhere near here. Time will be getting short by then.'

'Make it the beach,' Neil said. 'Just down by the open-air hot-dog stand.' He got to his feet. 'You won't let me down, will you?'

'I don't seem to have much choice.'

'No.' Neil stood, looking down at the boy. 'You know, Edward, you might try being a bit open-minded when you get to Oxford. Really go into it — see how a democracy really works. You might find your ideas get quite a shaking up.'

The superior smile was back in place.

'I know where I'm going,' Edward said, certainty in his voice. 'You just keep your promise to keep me out of it, and my future is assured.'

'Well, there's nothing more to be said, is there? I'll just wish you the best of Chinese luck, Edward old boy. Something tells me you're going to need it.'

Neil lifted his hand in a gesture of farewell and left Edward to his thoughts.

★   ★   ★

There wasn't much gaiety in the Wong ménage that night. Edward was invariably silent at meals and on this particular evening he took himself off to his room immediately they had finished. Marsha and Paul retreated to their sumptuous lounge and Marsha tried to read. Paul folded his hands over his pendulous stomach and meditated.

'You know he's seeing a girl, don't you?' he said at last. Marsha looked up at her husband, carefully marking her place in the magazine with a scarlet tipped finger.

'Who?'

'Who?' Paul echoed. 'Who? Edward, that's who. Your son. Don't you care?'

Marsha sighed. All too frequently now their domestic harmony was disrupted by futile discussions about their son's unsatisfactory nature. It had been all so pleasant when he was small, his character still unformed. They could fool themselves then with dreams of the future. But now Paul seemed obsessed by his disappointment in his son. Where she worried, he was outraged.

'Of course I care,' she said now. 'But he's eighteen, Paul. Didn't you expect girls?'

'Not like this one. I'm told she's a little nobody. She works in the Chinese Bank, Kee tells me.'

'Did Kee also tell you she's very pretty? Surely there's nothing wrong in a boy of eighteen having a date with a pretty girl.'

'I'll be glad when he leaves Hong Kong,' Wong said. 'I'm going to insist that he stays in Europe for Christmas. He could go skiing in Switzerland.'

'I don't suppose he'd object to that. Why don't you suggest it?'

'I said insist, not suggest. Why he can't show some interest in some of the suitable girls he's met, I can't imagine.'

'Oh, he will, I'm sure. As Sue Russell said to me the other day, all teenagers rebel against their parents. It's just a phase. He'll realise which side his bread is buttered on before he's much older. Yes Ying, what is it?'

The amah had come in on soundless feet

to announce a visitor and Paul Wong swore irritably. He was not the most social of creatures and hated surprise visits of any kind; when he saw the identity of the intruder he was even more angry and his plump face creased into an unwelcoming scowl.

'What do you want, Kee? State your business and get out.'

The visit boded nothing but ill. Kee had not been inside the house more than a handful of times in all the years that Wong had employed him. Marsha looked at him with a hostile, closed expression, knowing that his appearance had something to do with the house in Deepwater Bay and hating any taint of it to invade her home. Spending the profits from it was one thing; being forced to consider the mechanics of it quite another.

Kee wasted no time in small talk.

'This was found in the girl's room late this afternoon. It's just been handed to me.' He passed over a crumpled piece of paper.

Paul stretched out his hand to take it, looking at Kee enquiringly. 'Which girl are you talking about?'

'The one who killed herself.'

With a scowl, Paul took and read it. He stared at it in puzzled silence for a moment, then raised his head and looked at Marsha.

'It's the Russell girl's address,' he said.

'Susan Russell. And her telephone number.' He turned his eyes to Kee again. 'Why has it only just been found?'

'It was hidden, boss. The amah cleaned the room afterwards, but this wasn't found until the carpet was lifted to get at some wiring that needed attention.'

'Is this the number she was calling when you found her?'

Kee shrugged. 'I don't know. It could be.'

'You mean, you didn't find out?'

'She wouldn't talk.'

Paul laughed incredulously. 'And you couldn't make her? You must be losing your knack, Kee.'

'I would have returned to the job, you can be sure. How did I know she would drown herself in the meantime?'

Marsha shuddered delicately. 'Do we have to go into the details? It's much more important to think what this means — *oh*!' The memory of showing the bracelet to Sue came back to her in a blinding flash.

'What is it?' her husband asked.

'Nothing at all,' she said, unconvincingly.

Paul levered himself up from his chair and came over to sit next to her on the settee. She watched him apprehensively. God, she thought, what have I done? If Paul knew I'd so much as kept the bracelet, he'd kill me.

But what could be the link between those two girls? They were from completely different worlds — they would never have met, not in a million years. Yet Sue had been in Bangkok and the girl had owned a bracelet she had made, as well as being in possession of her address and telephone number.

'Marsha!' Paul's voice grated harshly. 'Marsha, you know something.'

'No, it's nothing. Nothing whatever to do with this.'

Wong turned to Kee. 'Would you leave us for a few moments?' he asked. 'Ying will find you some tea or beer or whatever you want. Wait in the library.'

He waited until the door had closed behind his employee before turning to his wife.

'Tell me,' he said simply.

'Paul, there's nothing to tell. Why are you looking at me like that? I was just astonished that Sue Russell could be known to that girl, that's all.'

'That's all, eh?'

'Absolutely.' She gave a light laugh, but it sounded false even to her own ears.

With a look that terrified her, knowing him as she did after twenty years of marriage, he leant forward and grabbed her wrist.

'Paul, stop it,' she said sharply. 'You're hurting me.'

'Not so much as I will hurt if you don't tell me the truth. You can't fool me, Marsha, I know you far too well. Now tell me what you know.'

'It's nothing important — really, you're making a great deal of fuss about nothing.' With any luck she could play it down. She would try anything to get Paul out of this mood. She had experienced it before on occasions and it terrified her.

'I'll tell you what I remembered so suddenly, if you'll stop behaving like a savage. That's better.' She rubbed her wrist and, having released it, Wong sat back with his arms folded, his eyes never leaving her face.

'It's simply that Sue happened to design the bracelet that the girl was wearing. It means nothing. She could have bought it anywhere. I only noticed it as it seemed a pretty piece of jewellery.'

'How do you know who designed it?'

'I guessed, that's all. You forget Sue showed me a selection of her designs. They were exactly the same — I mean, not all *exactly* the same, but of the same type. Anyone who knows anything about design could see they were done by the same person.'

'And my clever Marsha knew immediately? Where is it now?'

'Really Paul I've no idea.' Marsha's voice

was off-hand, but her husband was not deceived. She winced as once more he grasped her wrist.

'You kept it, didn't you? You *kept* it!'

Marsha licked her lips.

'Only so that I could explain the sort of thing I wanted from Sue for the shop. It was an exceptionally good bracelet, Paul.'

'Fool!'

Before Marsha could turn her head, he slapped her twice with the back of his hand, left and right. She turned away with a cry and buried her face in her hands, but he was not finished with her yet. He pulled one hand away and forced her to face him.

'You showed it to the Russell girl, didn't you?'

'Yes, yes, YES!' Marsha was crying now, streaks of mascara running down her face, and none of her friends would have recognised her as the poised, chic woman they knew. 'She was surprised to see it, but agreed it was one of her designs. There was nothing at all to make her suspicious.'

'Except that the little tramp from Bangkok had her address and telephone number. How?'

'I don't know. How could they have known each other?'

He flung her away from him in disgust and

strode out of the room to the library.

'Ring Petter,' he said tersely to Kee, who leapt to do his bidding.

'He's on the line, boss,' Kee told him, after a moment, and handed over the receiver.

'Good-evening, Petter.' Wong's voice was deceptively mild. 'I need some information.'

'Who is that? — oh!' Light had suddenly dawned on Chief Inspector Petter. 'It's you, Mr Wong. What can I do for you.'

'That young relative of mine who was found in Aberdeen harbour. You were able to play it down as instructed?'

'Oh yes, sir.' Petter was almost falling over himself in his desire to please. 'Absolutely no trouble at all.'

'No more developments?'

'No. It was a perfectly straightforward case.'

'Good.' Paul allowed himself to relax a little. 'It would have been embarrassing, you understand. A terrible blow to my old mother if the details had come out. I knew you'd understand.'

I'd understand most things, Petter thought, for the money-filled envelope that came at such regular intervals. It's not that he asks much, after all — nothing I can't square my conscience about. Of course his poor old mother would hate the publicity of a thing like this.

'No,' he said. 'It was an open-and-shut case.' He rather liked that term and repeated it with satisfaction. 'But it's well and truly shut now. It does seem, though, that your niece had a double somewhere. We had a young lady in swearing she was a girl she'd met in Bangkok.'

'And when was this?'

'Oh now, let me see.' Petter was blissfully unaware that Wong's anger was mounting with every passing second. He was not a sensitive man. 'It was early last week, I think, very shortly after she was found. She'd seen a picture and you know how easy it is to make a mistake! She thought — '

'The girl's name?' barked Wong.

'Pardon?'

'THE GIRL'S NAME!' Wong could hardly enunciate in his rage. He swallowed convulsively. 'What was the name of the girl who came into your office?'

'I can't remember,' Petter said nervously. 'Not without looking at the file. But I do remember she had that chap Neil Marriner with her — the one that writes in the Gazette. It was he who'd shown her a photograph of the dead girl.'

'Had he, indeed? I think that will be all,

thank you Mr Petter. Next time, kindly remember to give me *all* the information when I ask you. Remember who pays you.'

He slammed the phone down and stood, one hand fondling his chin, his brows knitted in thought. It was at this moment that Marsha entered hesitantly. Her husband looked at her, a look that made her wish she had kept well away.

'The Russell girl and Marriner went to the police-station to identify her,' he said. 'It seems I am surrounded by fools. Petter didn't report to me — he thought the matter had no significance.'

'What did he tell them?'

'The story I told him. It seems they were satisfied, at least according to Petter. How much I can rely on him I don't know. No doubt they were satisfied until you produced the bracelet. Now God alone knows what they think.'

'But Petter didn't say — I mean, no one has accused *us* of anything, have they?'

'Not yet.'

'How could anyone? We're covered, aren't we?' Her voice rose hysterically. 'You pay squeeze to all the right people, don't you? You've thought of every angle.'

'Except Marriner.'

Paul Wong walked heavily to the windows

and looked out over the vista spread before him — the formal gardens, the pool and beyond them the sea. It was a far cry from the squalid room in which he had spent his boyhood and he had no intention of losing the smallest of his material possessions.

'We'll have to close the operation,' he said. 'Make arrangements for all the girls to disperse. Sell the house. And Marsha — get out of my sight!'

'You really mean that, boss?' Kee asked incredulously when the door had shut behind her. 'You really mean to close? Have you seen the accounts for the last month? We're taking more than ever before, and there's another girl scheduled to arrive next week.'

Wong walked back to the centre of the room and sat down again at his desk, swivelling slightly from left to right, a small smile on his face.

'Of course not,' he said. 'That was for Marsha's benefit. The day that I let a nobody like Marriner get the better of me, you can bury me with my ancestors. You'll have to get rid of him, Kee — him and the girl. I don't believe there's anything I can't square with the police if they're left alone, but Marriner is a trouble-maker. He'll yap at their heels until they do something.'

Kee scratched his head dubiously. 'We

159

don't know how far they've gone, do we? If they've already caused a stir and then they disappear, the trail could lead straight to us.'

'You, Kee. You. Not me.'

'They're not nobodies, boss. People are going to ask questions if they wind up with a knife in their ribs in the harbour. It won't be like dealing with a couple of rickshaw-boys.'

Paul Wong moved petulantly in his chair. 'Use your brains, Kee. Get them well away from us — make it look like an accident, or a robbery or a kidnap or — anything at all, as long as you get *rid* of them.'

He thumped the desk with his clenched fist as he spoke and, with one look at his face, Kee left. If it had been within his power to feel sorry for anyone, he would certainly have felt sorry for Marsha. It would surprise him very considerably if Wong had finished with her yet.

8

The usual crowd, Bruno thought, looking round him without enthusiasm. Why he'd bothered to come he didn't know, except that a free drink was always nice and there was always the odd chance that one might meet a co-operative bird.

He looked across the room, glass in hand, to where Serena and Ian were standing with Lord Charman, greeting guests as they arrived. You've got to hand it to the Mandarin, Bruno thought. They do this kind of thing very well.

And he had to hand it to Serena too. She was charming everyone, as to the manner born. You could see that old Charman was lapping it up — he looked as if he thought she was the greatest thing since sliced bread.

Almost absently he put his empty glass on the tray of a passing waiter, slickly changing it for a full one. His gaze moved to Ian and his smile died. He was sick to the back teeth of hearing everyone say what a great guy he was. What the hell did he have, to make everyone acclaim him as such a paragon? He shook his head slowly in bewilderment. Where others saw integrity, he could only see smugness and it made no sense to him — in fact it sickened him.

He turned away to be faced by a sight which sickened him even more — Sue and Neil standing close together, engaged in animated conversation with a young couple who worked with Banstead Marvell. Even as he watched, Sue laughed at some comment made by Neil, who turned and looked down at her, giving her shoulder a wordless squeeze. No words were necessary and Bruno turned from them with a look of sardonic amusement. For a moment he hated them — both of them. He hated them for their obvious happiness and togetherness, for want of another word. He hated them because he knew he had far more to offer a girl than Neil Marriner; yet Sue had turned from him to Neil. He was glad now that he'd given Kee the information he'd been looking for. Even his conscience, hardened organ though it was, had suffered a twinge at first — not on Marriner's behalf — he had what was coming to him — but because of Sue. Why Wong wanted to know their movements he had no idea, but it obviously boded no good for Marriner, whom Wong had hated for months.

He took another drink from a passing tray and dismissed the thought of Kee in his office that morning, oily and persuasive with a fistful of hundred-dollar bills. He couldn't really believe that any harm would come to Sue, not with her connections. And as for Marriner — he knocked back best part of the contents of the glass and looked over once again to the merry knot of people in the corner. As for Marriner, he could go to hell.

* * *

It was all going reasonably well, Serena thought, her mind ticking over efficiently behind the smile. Lord Charman certainly seemed to be enjoying himself, but maybe Mrs Tollemache had been monopolising him for long enough and it was time for her to be moved on — in the nicest possible way, of course. She glanced at Ian, who got the message instantly, although engrossed in conversation with a top man from the Charter Bank. With the ease of long practice he moved in to introduce the bank man, while Serena executed a kind of pincer movement to cut off Mrs Tollemache.

'Do come and meet Mme Derrique from the French Embassy,' she said, smiling sweetly. 'You know Paris very well, don't you? She'll be so interested.'

With that manoeuvre completed, Serena

had time to look about her. Bruno, she noted, was looking more dispirited than usual — surely not because of Sue and Neil! She could not believe that his feelings had been seriously engaged, they never had been before. Just hurt pride, she told herself — and serve him right. She could see Paul Wong over there, laying down the law to some poor little man, a very lowly member of the Banstead Marvell staff. Marsha was not present. Indisposed, Paul had said, but Serena didn't really believe that. She felt it was more likely that Marsha was staging a protest about the way she had been dropped from Serena's closest circle. Well, too bad, Serena thought. Marsha was too much a part of that pre-Ian life she was trying to forget.

The decibel level increased by the minute. With any luck, Serena thought, Lord Charman wouldn't want to stay too long — then a quiet dinner, a trip to the airport and they would be shot of him. It had been a tough two days for Ian, but as always he gave no sign of it. He was as strong as a horse, in spite of the fact he was so thin.

She was proved sadly wrong about Lord Charman. He had every intention of staying just as long as possible, to the the point where dinner was rushed and the drive to the airport a race against time. It was with a sigh of relief that they saw him amble amiably into the First Class departure lounge.

'I haven't had a minute to talk to you all day,' Ian said, on the way back.

'No.' Serena yawned. 'He's not a bad old stick, though, is he? Do you think you'll still be dashing round the world, living it up, when you're his age?'

'Serena, there's something I've got to tell you — something we have to decide between us.'

Serena's heart tripped as it always did when Ian sounded so serious. She never was sure what he was going to say — what he had found out.

'What is it?' she asked now.

'Just that B.M. want me to take over Australia. It seems it's in a mess and I've got the reputation of being a trouble-shooter. It's a bigger job, of course — quite a challenge really, because this chap Collins who has been there upset all kinds of apple-carts. The trade with Japan is down to its lowest level ever, but the potential is enormous.'

'Oh Ian, that's marvellous!'

'But you'll hate leaving Hong Kong — and I hate asking you to.'

'That's ridiculous! I expected to move — oh, not yet, perhaps, but eventually. Anyway, I'll welcome it.'

'You will?'

'Of course. A new challenge, a fresh start. I bet there's a super house to go with it, isn't there?'

Ian laughed. 'I expect so — I didn't ask.'

'When do they want you?'

'Quite soon. Before Christmas.'

'Heavens above! That *is* moving.'

'You're sure you don't mind?' Ian glanced across at his wife, seeing her face illuminated by a glaring green sign. 'Charman did say that they'd understand any reluctance on my part, as I'd been here such a short time.'

'There's no reluctance on my part, darling.' Serena put her head back on the seat and closed her eyes blissfully. It had to happen of course, one day. She had known that inevitably Ian would be moved on — but had never expected it so soon. It was the answer to everything. In a new country there would be no shadow of the past hanging over her and she could truly begin again.

She gave a gurgle of laughter. 'Will you mind our children having Aussie accents?'

'Not a bit.' Ian smiled down at her. 'You'd better make it soon, though, or I shall be too old to enjoy playing with their trains.'

'You'll never be too old, sport,' his wife told him, with a fair approximation of an Australian accent herself.

Ian smiled down at her. 'Maybe not — not with you around.' He smiled out at the street with its covered-over stalls and the neon signs meeting almost overhead.

'I shall miss this place though, won't you? In a way I'm sorry to leave.'

'I'm not.' At her flat denial he smiled down at her again protectively, but said nothing. He never had — and please God, he never would.

★   ★   ★

Neil and Sue had arranged an early start on Saturday for the trip to Cheung Chau. Sue had been looking forward to it so much that she felt an almost fatalistic certainty that something would happen to prevent it. The weather would have broken, a typhoon would be incubating somewhere in the South China Sea or Neil's editor would have found some urgent task for him that could not possibly be postponed. But none of these disasters had come to pass and secure in the circle of Neil's arm she looked through eyes starry with happiness at the islands in front of them. They were near enough now to see the colour-washed buildings that began in a thick cluster round the skirt of the island and dwindled in number as the road rose higher.

They could see activity on the quay-side — market-stalls and hurrying figures, a cluster of sampans at the jetty.

'Hong Kong must have looked like this seventy years ago,' Sue said. She was leaning forward, her folded arms on the cabin roof. 'Yet there's a sort of Mediterranean look about it, don't you agree? It looks as if it's been painted in oils by one of the impressionists.'

'I see what you mean,' Neil agreed. 'But wait until you're on dry land. It's really totally Chinese — far more so than Hong Kong is now. You'll see more odd-looking food along that quayside than you've had hot dinners.'

'Serena was telling me about a festival they have here in the Spring.'

'Yes — the Bun Festival, it's called, though I've never understood quite why because the buns they eat aren't really buns at all. It's a happy sort of occasion. I'll bring you to the next one.'

Sue took time out from her study of the island to turn round and look at him quizzically. So far there had been nothing put into words about the length of her stay or of their relationship as a whole. Her date of departure was still comfortably vague, though with Serena and Ian dashing off to Sydney during the next couple of months this was a state of affairs which obviously couldn't continue. Still, her journey home was not yet imminent and therefore not nearly as important as this exciting voyage of discovery they had mutually undertaken, with no distant island as the prize but rather an intimate understanding of each other. There was, however, no time to investigate the full implications of his remark now. The sea traffic was thickening and Neil needed both hands and all his concentration to bring the junk safely to anchor at a point not far from the jetty. A sampan, sculled with a single oar from the stern by a tiny woman in pink cotton trousers and tunic, almost entirely extinguished by a huge coolie hat, detached itself from the cluster of boats and approached them swiftly with an offer to ferry them to the shore.

There was a brisk and good-humoured exchange in Cantonese.

'I'm making it quite clear I'm not a tourist,' Neil said. 'That means I halve the price she suggests, subtract another dollar, and then maybe we arrive somewhere near the actual going rate for the job.'

By this means or some other, agreement was eventually reached and after making sure that any possessions were safely locked in the cabin they clambered down into the sampan and were soon standing on the quay-side.

The whole atmosphere fascinated Sue. Here was a small fishing community, the essence of which had probably been changed very little since the turn of the century. There had been changes, of course. Here and there were stark new buildings and further up the hill were newer and more impressive houses, but here in the little town it seemed as if they had been transported back to another age, pre-skyscraper and pre-pneumatic drill.

They wandered hand-in-hand through the local shoppers, all of whom seemed to find it necessary to communicate with each other in harsh, staccato shouts. They stopped, over and over again, to look at the stalls that were ranged along the side of the quay. There was much that was cheap and tawdry.

'A plethora of plastic,' Neil announced. 'And why so many lavatory brushes, in heaven's name? They're all over the place. Anyone would think that the lavatories of Cheung Chau were the cleanest in the world, whereas I can assure you from my own experience — '

'Say no more,' Sue begged. 'Leave me with some illusions. The basketwork is lovely, you must admit. Shall I buy a hat?'

'Tripper!' Neil laughed at her — but she bought one just the same.

They turned into an alley that gave on to a narrow, dark street and even more strongly Sue experienced the sensation of going back in time. Here the shops were full of mysteries. There were herbalists with things in jars that looked like pickled snakes or frogs — strange, exotic things that hinted of necromancy. There were trestles outside a food-shop with rows of raw, shelled eggs drying in the sun, looking for all the world like halves of tinned peaches. There were jewellers and lantern-shops and fire-cracker-shops — and over all the insistent clatter of the Mah Jong tiles coming from behind closed doors. The games never stopped, it seemed. Sue wondered if the same people played all the time — or was there always someone waiting to take the place of a player who dropped out through sheer exhaustion? Whatever happened, the clatter never ceased.

They arrived eventually at the temple. Worshippers were bringing food to place before the shrines. Neil and Sue stood to one side and watched them as totally absorbed they lit their joss-sticks and bowed and muttered before the particular shrine they seemed to favour.

'What's the food for?' Sue whispered.

'Their ancestors.'

'But what happens to it? Is it all wasted?'

'The Chinese are far too practical for that. I think they take it all away again — it's the thought that counts!'

'I'm so ignorant, Neil. If I were going to stay here, I'd want to learn everything. What it all means — what they believe.'

Neil swung her around and headed back to the street and the fish restaurant where they were to eat lunch. 'You'll stay,' he said with mock toughness. 'I'll personally undertake your education — and I don't mean only in the field of Eastern religions.'

It was still a joke. But it seemed to Sue that the possibility of a future together was something that intrigued both of them. They both flirted with the thought, toyed with it, kicked it around in their minds.

There was a heart-stopping sweetness in the thought of belonging to someone. Yet they had known each other such a short time and to commit themselves they needed to be sure. For some reason, nothing less than a permanent relationship entered her mind where Neil was concerned; it would be that or it would be nothing.

'I have an idea,' Neil said. He was sitting back in his chair after the excellent lunch, feeling replete and well content with life. He reached across and took Sue's hand.

'Like what?'

'Like — attractive though this island is, there are too many damned people on it. Why don't we up anchor and find us a nice little bay where we can swim in privacy? We can always come back here another day.'

'Suits me. We've done a tour of the town, haven't we? Is there much more to see?'

'There are beaches, but they'll all be crowded today. Maybe it was a tactical error choosing Saturday afternoon.'

'Let's go, then.'

Neil settled the bill, which to Sue seemed surprisingly low for the amount they had eaten, and they made their way back to the jetty. The sampan-lady in the pink cotton greeted them joyously and ferried them back to the junk, now rapidly taking on the appearance of an old friend. Sue was now sufficiently practised to take an active part in preparing for moving off. We make a good team, she thought — but it was not a thought she would have uttered aloud; merely a small, private satisfaction.

By the time she had returned to the rear deck Neil had stripped down to swimming-trunks and she too lost no time in taking off the cotton skirt and blouse that she had put on for decency's sake while walking round the streets of Cheung Chau.

She went down into the cabin to fetch the

foam cushions and, feeling comfortably lethargic, she stretched out in the shade, strategically positioning it on the deck so that behind the slits of her half-closed eyes she could still see Neil at the helm. He was whistling softly to himself as he steered away from Cheung Chau towards a group of smaller islands that lay on their starboard bow. His legs were braced against the stately dip and rise of the elderly junk, and Sue smiled because he looked just as she felt; that God was in his heaven and all was right with the world.

They had passed a string of islands on their way to Cheung Chau, some more hospitable-looking than others. Now they went a little out of their way to find one with a sheltered bay that would be perfect for their swim.

'It's got to be right,' Neil said, dismissing one where the weed seemed too thick. 'We'll take a look at that one over there.'

'That's a strange-looking boat,' Sue said, pointing back the way they had come. 'It almost seems to be shadowing us.'

Neil gave a brief glance over his shoulder. 'You get all sorts of peculiar-looking craft out at weekends,' he said. 'Look, this seems perfect — what do you say? The water's incredibly clear.'

They dropped anchor and Neil came to sit

on the second cushion beside her. 'Maybe we should rest a while before swimming,' he said. 'That was some meal, wasn't it?'

Sue agreed sleepily. 'I'm sure I'd sink like a stone.'

He stretched out beside her, propping himself on an elbow as he studied her face, tracing with his finger the curve of her mouth.

'What's going to happen to us, Sue?'

'Isn't it a little soon to know?'

He bent and kissed her, briefly. 'I suppose so. Reason says so. But somehow I don't think that reason has a lot to do with it.'

They studied each other for a moment in silence, then she stretched up her arms to him and he came into them, holding her close now in a kiss that seemed as if it would never end.

The sound of a powerful boat engine forced itself upon their consciousness and Neil groaned.

'Oh, not again! There's no peace any-where.'

'Just ignore it,' Sue said. 'Maybe it'll go away.' But the beat of the engine came nearer and now they could hear shouts, sharp and authoritative.

'What the hell do they want?' Reluctantly Neil got to his feet and went to look over the side, followed by Sue who was only fractionally behind him. She was totally unprepared for his cry of alarm and the way in which he pushed her down on to the deck as a line of bullets ripped into the hull just above the waterline.

The boat had by this time drawn alongside, hull to hull, and Neil's face was a study in total bewilderment as he looked at its grey paint and the flag with the red sun of China flying from the stern. Two grey-uniformed figures were preparing to climb aboard the junk, both armed with sub-machine-guns.

'What the hell do you think you're doing? Keep off this boat! We're in British waters here.' Neil looked wildly round. Where now were the odd pleasure craft that they had seen at each step of the way? There was not one to be seen.

The only reply from their attackers was a burst of Chinese, incomprehensible to Sue, but with the two guns directed towards them at such short range the meaning was all too clear. They took no notice whatsoever of Neil's protests and climbed aboard the junk prodding them and gesturing with their guns for them to go down into the Chinese boat.

'This is ridiculous,' Neil argued furiously. 'We're nowhere near your territorial waters.'

'You in Chinese waters. You and girl, both

spies.' The soldier that had spoken appeared to be grinning, though, as time went on and his expression never changed, Sue later decided that his face was just built that way.

'Of course we're not spies! We're just out for a swim, that's all, on our way from Cheung Chau to Hong Kong. I can show you the exact spot on the chart.'

'You spies. This China.'

Exasperatedly Neil turned to Sue. 'This is crazy! I *know* where we are.'

'What do they want us to do?' Her teeth, she found, had suddenly begun to chatter. She had never been more terrified.

'Go with them, it appears.' He turned to the soldiers again and began to speak to them in Cantonese. Throughout they remained impassive and Sue could only assume that he was going over the same ground again. If so, it was to no avail. All Neil could win from them was a chance to put their outer clothes on again; beyond that, they would accept no argument. Neil and Sue were to descend from the junk into the Chinese boat and, with those guns levelled at them so menacingly, there seemed little argument that would be effective.

It was a strangely old-fashioned-looking boat they were herded into, about forty feet in length with a cabin below decks. Every inch of it was painted a uniform gun-metal-grey. There were no guns actually mounted on it, but there was a military air about it, enhanced by the three figures in their grey uniforms and peaked caps.

The engine was surprisingly powerful, Neil thought, and wondered what kind it was. There was no way he could see, since they had both been forced down into the cabin with the hatch battened down. The portholes had been obscured with grey paint and only a dim light filtered through to them.

'At least,' Neil said, as they roared off, presumably in an easterly direction, 'there will surely be an officer we can talk to, whenever we get to wherever they're taking us. I can't believe he won't listen to us. I swear they've made a mistake. I know where all the Chinese islands are and this wasn't one of them.'

Sue was sitting with her back against the bulkhead on a narrow, bench-like seat that ran around the sides of the cabin. Neil came and sat beside her, putting his arm around her.

'Darling, I'm so sorry,' he said. 'But don't be frightened. I know it's a mistake — it *has* to be. We'll be free in no time, once we can talk to someone with a bit of sense.'

The shock of the whole incident had

banished coherent thought from Sue's mind. One moment, it seemed, they had been kissing in the sun — the next they were battened down in this hole, guarded by three soldiers and two guns. She struggled hard against an overwhelming feeling of panic, clutching Neil to her with icy-cold hands.

'What — what do they do to spies?' she asked, not liking the quaver of fear she could detect in her voice.

'That won't arise.' Neil spoke with certainty.

'It's horrible not being able to see, isn't it? We seem to be going miles. Where do you think they're taking us, Neil?'

'I suppose some port in China.' He tried to recall the geography of that particular region. 'Or maybe to one of the Chinese islands.'

There was no possible way in which they could gain even a rough idea of the direction in which they were heading and nothing they could do but to sit with their hands clasped, trying not to let their imaginations run riot.

'Things have changed an awful lot,' Neil said at one point. 'Since Mao's been gone, China's attitude to the outside world is changing all the time. Years ago, we might have been in danger, but not now.'

'Then why, if things are easier, do they do things like this?'

'Because these moronic bastards don't know what they're doing.'

Sue shivered and immediately Neil's arms were round her again.

'Cold?' he asked.

'Not really. Just scared stiff.'

'Hold on, darling. Everything will be all right.'

They huddled together finding little more to say until the reduced beat of the engine caused them to draw apart curiously.

'We're stopping, I think,' Neil said.

'Do you know the Chinese for 'Take me to your Leader'?' Sue asked, as they both stood up.

'I'll manage.'

The boat came to rest, bumping against the side of a quay or jetty, and after a few moments the hatchway was thrown open and the smaller of the two men equipped with guns was revealed. He gestured with his weapon for them to go outside.

Curiously they looked about them as they emerged on deck. They were in a thickly wooded bay. They were moored to a slatted wooden jetty, old and rickety and looking as if it had been many months since any craft had tied up there. Over at the far side of the bay was a cluster of peasant cottages. There were no other boats and no more soldiers, other than the three that had been with them all the time. A narrow, winding path led up the steep cliff and towards this they were pushed with a great deal of shouting and threatening gestures with the guns.

Apparently unconcerned, Neil stood his ground and spoke to them. Sue assumed he was repeating his demand to see an officer, but his calm, courteous voice seemed only to annoy them and it was with a vicious jab of the gun that the smiling soldier forced him round towards the cliff.

'We walk. You go,' he shouted.

One of the soldiers, carrying a gun, led the way, followed by Sue with Neil close behind her. The one unarmed soldier came next and the third soldier with his gun, brought up the rear. The path was only wide enough to allow one person to pass at a time. Bushes pressed in on both sides and caught at Sue's skirt. It was very steep and after a very short time Sue could feel herself labouring. She slowed her pace, which in turn slowed Neil, so that the soldier behind him punched him savagely in the back.

'You go, you go,' he shouted. 'Go fast.'

'The lady can't walk as quickly as you,' Neil said. 'We're going as fast as we can.'

'Walk!' The third soldier holding the gun changed places with the second, so that now any slackening of pace would mean that the butt would be jammed between Neil's shoulder-blades. Half-sobbing, Sue continued, trying to keep up a good pace. She was desperately frightened now. This seemed such a wild and lonely place.

The walk seemed endless. Eventually they reached the top of the cliff but there still seemed no sign of their destination, neither were there cultivated fields or water-buffalo. Neil checked his watch. They had been walking for over twenty minutes now at a rapid pace and there had been no evidence of habitation. He had no idea where they could have landed.

In only a few more minutes they were out of the thick bushes and had emerged on a grassy plain, but all too soon they had plunged into woodland again and were once more climbing upwards.

'I can't stand much more of this,' gasped Sue, stopping in her tracks and leaning against a tree. They were actually permitted to rest for a few moments and were then herded upwards again.

The trees were getting thinner and Neil felt certain that they must have been nearing their destination. He was unprepared, however, for the shock of finding they had actually arrived; that there, where the trees grew more sparse and finally petered out altogether, were some huts, set roughly in a square, up on stilts with a verandah round each one.

It looked vaguely like an army camp, but if so it was the oddest one that Neil had ever seen. For one thing, there were no other soldiers there, it appeared; and, for another, there was a strange air of desolation about the place. Some of the huts seemed almost derelict, with sagging roofs and broken windows. Their footsteps slowed as they approached it.

'There's no one here,' Neil said softly, coming alongside Sue and taking her arm. 'What the hell's going on?' He stopped and looked back at the guard behind them, demanding yet again to speak to an officer.

In reply, the two sub-machine-guns were levelled again, and Neil swallowed convulsively, his mouth suddenly dry. He reached for Sue's hand. Surely this was a nightmare. The whole of the civilised world seemed to have withdrawn from them, leaving them alone and helpless and miles from home. He no longer felt quite so certain that they would be on their way back as soon as he explained the situation — the main stumbling-block being that there was no one but these three goons to explain to. Nevertheless he continued to try.

'You'll be in trouble for this,' he said. 'We are innocent people. The chairman will be displeased when the western press hear of this.'

Still smiling, the short man at last spoke.

'You wait,' he said. 'You go in there and wait.' He indicated a room on one side of the square and herded them towards it, pushing them roughly up the steps to the verandah. There were two rooms in this one block, both opening out on to the verandah. One was securely padlocked, but the other stood open and they were pushed inside.

It was about ten feet square, bare except for two iron bedsteads, their springs covered by thin mattresses. The walls were clean and there was a smell of paint in the air as if they had only recently been decorated, but the floor was concrete, pitted and in bad repair. A thin brown blanket was neatly folded on each mattress and this, apart from a swinging, empty light socket, was the sum total of the furnishings in the room.

'You wait,' their guard said again.

'Wait how long? You can't keep us here!'

Neil's words echoed hollowly. Who was to stop them? He, Sue and their Chinese guards knew that there was nothing the prisoners could possibly do.

'I not know how long. Maybe one day,

maybe two. Here are beds for sleeping.' He prodded the beds with his gun as if they might have escaped their attention. 'We bring you food later. You want ablutions, you tell guard.'

'I want ablutions,' Sue said quickly.

'Me too.' Neil's voice was hard and angry, but he had received the message loud and clear; the Chinese were quite immovable and it would do no good at all to bluster and make demands. Better to save it until someone in authority came — whenever that was likely to be.

Silently he stood by the nearer bed as one of the guards, his gun levelled as always, shepherded Sue from the room and across the courtyard to a shower-block which apparently stood at the end. He exchanged no words with his guard while she was gone and in a few moments she was back and it was his turn to make the short journey.

'All right?' he asked briefly as he passed her.

'Foul,' she replied, equally briefly.

On his return, they were locked in securely and left alone. Neil prowled round the room examining windows and doors, watched by Sue who sat on one of the beds.

'What are our chances of breaking out?' she asked him.

Neil came and sat down beside her. 'It doesn't look too difficult — but to what end, I ask myself? There's a guard standing lower down at the open end of the courtyard, but quite apart from that I wouldn't know where to make for. No one is let out of China easily, you know, even their own nationals. What puzzles me is — what is the place? Where is everyone, if it's an army camp?'

'Could it be a sort of summer camp?'

'Maybe. Did you notice, Sue, before we came in this room, that we're not really as far from civilisation as it would seem from that ghastly cross-country hike we did? There was quite a good road leading down the hill from this camp to what looked like a village.'

'So what do we do?'

Neil was silent. 'I suppose, just wait for the time being. I haven't any instant solutions — I still think we've got nothing to fear, once we can talk to someone intelligent.'

'Still, I'm frightened.'

'Who wouldn't be? I hate this place — it gives me the shivers.'

Sue looked around her. 'It seems reasonably clean.' She rubbed at the ticking of the mattresses thoughtfully. 'Do you suppose the beds have bugs?'

'Probably!'

'Thank heaven they've put us together.'

'That compensation had occurred to me.'

The door was flung open and one of their captors came in carrying two bowls of rice and two glasses of green tea on a tin tray. Without a word, he put this on the floor at their feet and slammed out of the room again.

'Dinner, I take it, is served.' Neil bent down and handed one of the bowls to Sue. 'We even have the refinement of chopsticks.'

Sue prodded doubtfully at the cooling mess in the bowl.

'What is it, do you think?' She sniffed and answered her own question. 'Fish, I imagine.'

They ate a little, but neither had much appetite for the unappetising fare. The tea was refreshing and surprisingly good, however, and the entire meal — unsatisfactory though it had been — restored some sort of balance to Sue's outlook. Neil was right, of course. They were held captive and not in the most comfortable surroundings, but they were not in any immediate danger.

The room grew darker as the shadows lengthened. Neil looked at his watch and wondered what the drill would be once Ian realised that his sister had not returned from her day out. Would he alarm the coast-guard? If so, the abandoned junk would be found together with the tell-tale bullet-holes in the hull. Heaven alone knew what they would think — and heaven alone could imagine his friend John's language should the junk not be restored to him. A poor thing it might be, but it was his pride and joy. Neil sighed heavily. One could only hope it was well insured.

'I wonder what Ian and Serena will think.' Out of the gathering darkness Sue spoke as if divining the direction of his thoughts. 'They'll be so worried.'

'I've absolutely got to get out before Monday.'

'Oh, your meeting with Edward! Yes, of course you must. But that's not until the day after tomorrow, for heaven's sake — surely we'll be home before then.'

Neil said nothing. The darkness grew and filled the room. He went to the window and looked out. Across the square the glint of metal caught his eye and he became aware that the guard was still there, still with his gun at the ready. At that moment one of the other soldiers came out of the hut opposite and light spilled over the brown and beaten earth of the courtyard, illuminating the one spindly tree in an overgrown bed in the centre.

'This is a weird place,' Neil said again. 'I swear no one's been here for ages.

The two soldiers were talking. It was the changing of the guard, it appeared. The smiling one went back to the room, leaving his replacement outside.

'Blast it,' Neil said, bitterly. 'I need those ghastly ablutions again.'

He hammered on the window, bringing the guard over at a run. Having communicated his needs, the same routine as before was observed before they were once again battened down for the night. Sue went over to the window to see the guard taking up his position at the end of the block.

'Someone's got to say it,' Neil said, putting his arm round her.

'Say what?'

'Alone at last!' He held her and moved his lips against her hair. 'How do you feel about spending the night with me?'

'The conditions are hardly ideal — but I think I've regarded it for some time now as inevitable in the long run.'

Neil closed his eyes. But we might only have a short run, he thought. Please God, let us live. Let us get out of here. And please, please, let me make her happy.

Dawn was breaking before they slept. It had been a night of revelation, with love-making interspersed with talk, with confidences, with seemingly pointless reminiscences and observations. Can any human being really know another? Neil asked himself, as propped on one elbow he looked down into Sue's still and dreaming face. Perhaps not — yet he felt that they had come close to it that night.

He loved her. He had admitted the possibility of loving her as far back as the first evening of their meeting, but had been misled by all the gossip about Bruno. She was, he had thought then, the loveliest girl he had ever seen. She was even lovelier now.

9

Ian settled himself more comfortably into his chair and sighed with pleasure. An evening at home with his wife was something to be treasured — an all too infrequent pleasure these days. It was not likely to be any better in his new job either. Still, it was all part of the game and, if there were times when the social round seemed pointless, he was only too well aware there were also times when an invaluable contact had been made at a cocktail-party or a thorny problem solved over a drink rather than an expanse of office desk. All in all, he was well content. He knew he did a good job for the company and it was satisfactory, to say the least, that they realised it. It was lucky for him that Serena was such an expert in her rôle.

He looked across at her now and smiled. With bare feet tucked up on the sofa under her caftan and her hair tied in a knot on the top of her head, she looked about sixteen. A daughter like that might be nice. Did she mean it, he wondered? That remark about children? With his mind busy with family matters, he naturally thought of his sister.

'What time do you expect Sue?' he asked.

Serena looked up from her book. 'I haven't a clue. She has a key and said don't wait up. She's out with Neil Marriner, you know.'

'Yes. I'm pleased about that.'

'They seemed — ' Serena broke off, a thoughtful look on her face. 'They seemed — I don't know. Very taken up with each other.'

'At the party last night? Yes, I thought so too.'

'You think they suit each other.'

Ian laughed. 'I don't think it matters much what I think — but for what it's worth, yes. I think they have much the same outlook on life.'

Serena returned to her book. 'Well, anyone would be better than Bruno.'

The companionable silence between them lasted for a few minutes, then Ian lifted his head.

'There's a car coming,' he said. 'Sue must be home earlier than she thought.'

A car door slammed and a doorbell pealed. The servants had gone off duty and Ian went to answer it, returning moments later with Bruno himself. His hair was wild and there was a strange, greyish tinge to his complexion.

'Sorry to burst in,' he was saying to Ian.

'But I need help — badly. God, I'm in the most awful trouble! I couldn't think of anyone to turn to except you.'

Serena put her book down again and studied him coolly.

'What's wrong?' she asked.

'Just about everything. Can I have a drink?'

'Sure.' Ian went to the drinks cabinet and poured him a sizeable tot of whisky. 'Water?'

'No, just ice.' Bruno drank half the contents of the glass in one gulp and sat down on the edge of the sofa next to Serena, nursing the rest between his hands. 'I'll be glad to be spared any lectures,' he said defensively. 'I always knew there was a risk and I weighed up the odds and decided to take it.'

'Just what is the trouble?' Ian asked.

'The I.C.A.C. is the trouble. They're on to me.'

'For doing what?' Serena's voice was cold. Bruno rounded on her. 'For God's sake don't be so blasted innocent! You know I couldn't have lived my sort of life-style on the legitimate proceeds of the business — I *had* to make something on the side. But what I've only just realised is that Wong was using me as a fall-guy. We were supposed to be in business together, dealing with quotas. That part of it was OK — I understood it, more or less; but you know me, Serena. I haven't a clue about accounts. I took far too much on trust and Wong played me for a complete sucker over all sorts of other deals. Now, when we're investigated, it leaves him whiter than white and me covered in crap.'

'How do you know about this?'

'Well, Sue warned me first.'

'*Sue?*'

'Yeah — Marriner told her. He'd heard some sort of rumour. I dismissed the whole thing — well, I thought then that Wong would see me right, but it's not that way at all. He's planned it so that everything falls right in my lap.'

'Oh Bruno, you really are the most idiotic — '

'Shut *up*, Serena!'

Ian looked at his brother-in-law with something like pity in his eyes. This sort of situation was something he could never in a million years imagine getting into himself — but he recognised a sucker when he saw one and had no doubt that, venal as Bruno undoubtedly was, in this particular case he had been more sinned against than sinning.

'What do you want me to do?' he asked now.

'Look — I'll cut my losses and go.' Bruno spoke urgently, leaning forward towards Ian.

'My information is that they'll seal up my office tomorrow and start going through the books — so my only chance is to leave tonight. I — I couldn't stand a prison sentence — I'd go mad. I'd rather lose everything and start again.'

'Most of your worldly goods are on the never-never anyway,' Serena commented dryly.

'I own the yacht,' he argued hotly. 'And the car'

'So what do you want me to do?' Ian asked again, patiently.

'I need money — enough for a passage to London. There's a plane leaving around midnight and I could get on that, if I could finance it.'

'Use your credit cards,' Serena said dryly.

Bruno looked embarrassed. 'I can't do that,' he said. 'There was some mix-up — just a mistake, of course, but they've withdrawn credit.' He looked at Ian. 'Banstead Marvell must have an account somewhere for travel purposes, surely? Maybe you could just make a phone call and fix me up.'

A feeling of outrage began to simmer quietly inside the usually calm breast of Ian. 'I don't operate that way,' he said. 'And I've very little cash in the house. But I'll give you a cash cheque and you can change it at the airport. Will that do?'

'That'll be great.' Bruno sagged with relief, but not before Serena spoke to him, her voice low with anger.

'How *dare* you come here, expecting Ian to be as rotten as you are? You are just about the most despicable thing I've ever seen. When things are going well for you, you come and sneer at our so-called respectable way of life — the fact that Ian is upright and honest and everyone thinks well of him. You make fun of me, because I don't want any part of your way of life. You — '

'Shut *up!*' Bruno's face was livid with anger as he turned to face Serena. 'Of course I make fun of you, you silly bitch — flaunting yourself round this house like a duchess when you know and I know and everyone in Hong Kong knows you'd fall into bed at the drop of a hat, in the good old days. Or perhaps I should say, at the rustle of a few dollars.'

'That's enough.' Ian had been on his feet, almost out of the room on his way to fetch his cheque-book. Now he stopped and looked, ice-cold, towards his brother-in-law. 'You've said enough, Bruno.'

Bruno stood too, breathing heavily. He licked his lips, trying to assess whether he had just talked himself out of getting a cheque from Ian. 'I'm sorry,' he said. 'I didn't mean it, of course.'

'Just watch your tongue.' Ian went out to the study and brother and sister were left alone. Serena was chalk-white — but it was Bruno's eyes that dropped first. Ian found them silent when he returned.

He held out a cheque to Bruno. 'Here,' he said. 'I hope it's enough.'

Bruno took it and looked at the amount. 'That — that really is most generous of you. Of course, it's just a loan. I'll pay it back once I'm on my feet.'

'Please don't bother.' Ian's voice was still icy-cold. 'Regard it as a gift. I only lend money to friends. You can see yourself out, can't you?'

'Yes — yes, of course.' Bruno stood indecisively, looking from one of them to the other. 'Well, thanks again. I really am very grateful.' Neither made any reply.

He looked towards Serena. 'Goodbye, sis.'

She nodded stonily, but said nothing, and after another moment Bruno shrugged and made for the door.

'Just one thing,' Ian said, stopping him in his tracks just before he reached it. Bruno looked back enquiringly. 'You will make sure that's a one-way ticket, won't you?'

Bruno looked at him for a moment and left

quickly. They heard the sound of his car as it drove away and listened in silence until the noise of the engine had faded completely.

'I shouldn't have said that,' Ian said at last.

Serena made no reply. When Ian looked at her, he saw that she was crying, slow tears pouring down her cheeks. He went to her and put his arms round her.

'I love you,' he said.

'How can you possibly?'

'I just do.'

'I hoped you'd never know about me.'

He held her against his shoulder and stroked her hair. 'I've known from the beginning — or almost from the beginning. You don't think that in a place this small I wouldn't hear about your background, do you? All sorts of people were at great pains to tell me.'

'And you didn't mind?'

'Of course I minded: I tried to forget you. I stayed away for two whole weeks, don't you remember? And I missed you like hell and wanted you so, I just couldn't bear it.'

'I'm not the same person any more. Darling, you must believe me. I love you so.'

'I know you do. And I love you and that's all that matters — not what other people think I ought to feel or what you were like years ago before we met. Now just listen to me.'

'Mm?'

Serena sniffed and raised her blurry, tear-stained face to him.

'I will not have you wearing a hair-shirt over this for the rest of our days. I know you wish it had been different. We all regret things. My God, I do! I've said hurtful things to people — like just now, to Bruno. Fancy telling him not to come back! What good does that do? I've probably made him more sure than ever that I'm a pompous, pious prig instead of demonstrating to him that our way is best after all. God knows I didn't mean it! It just seemed a good exit line.'

'Bruno deserved it — and so do I. You should tell me the same.'

But her arms were twined round his neck as if it would take more than words to make her go. He bent to kiss her, but the telephone bell interrupted him.

'Damn' thing,' he grumbled. 'Unhand me, woman — I must go and answer it. Don't go away though, will you?'

From the study she could hear the sound of his voice raised in anger or surprise and lifted her head to listen with a frown. Who on earth could it be, this time of night? Surely not more trouble with Bruno.

He was back in the sitting-room in only a few moments, his expression distraught.

'It's Sue,' he said hoarsely. 'Sue and Neil. They've been kidnapped.'

'*Kidnapped!*' Serena ran to him, holding his arms and looking up at him. 'What — who — '

'Somebody — a Chinese — just phoned to tell me, demanding a ransom. He said he'd already phoned Vaughan of the 'Gazette', demanding a quarter of a million dollars jointly for both of them. There were all sorts of conditions — we weren't to tell the police, the notes were to be put in a suitcase and left in the lobby of the Hong Kong Hotel on Monday morning, they were to be of small denominations, the usual sort of thing.' The phone rang again. 'That'll be Vaughan now, I should think.'

He disengaged himself from Serena and was back at the telephone with a few rapid strides. As he had guessed, the editor was at the other end of the line. They exchanged a few terse sentences before Ian put the phone down.

'He's already contacted the Secretary for Security.'

'But they said don't tell the police!'

'He's above the police. I agree with him, Serena, we had to tell someone. We're going to meet in the Secretary's flat now.'

'Can I come? Please, Ian; I don't want to stay here alone.'

'Get some clothes on quickly then.'

'This is extraordinary,' she said, when they were on their way. 'It's never happened here. Italy, yes — but not Hong Kong.'

'They're learning the ways of the Western barbarians.' Ian's voice was savage as he wrenched the wheel round the curves of the road to town. In front of them, as always, was the gaudy sprawl of Kowloon and as always the eye was inexorably drawn towards it. On this occasion, however, it was not the brightness that struck him, but the immensity of the area, the sheer size of the number of dwellings that must have been contained within it.

They could be anywhere.

10

'I'm going to see if I can have a shower.' Sue rapped imperiously on the window and the guard eventually heard and came over, unlocking the door cautiously and entering the small room with his gun levelled at them.

'Shower!' she demanded, making washing motions and pointing towards the ablutions at the end of the block.

The guard slammed the door and left them, but only for a few minutes. To their surprise he was back in a very short time, holding a cake of highly scented pink soap.

'Thank you,' Sue said, in some amazement. She pulled a 'see what a clever girl I am' face at Neil and marched off with the guard as escort.

Not surprisingly, the water was icy-cold, but once the initial shock had passed she found it had a restorative effect and she felt much more optimistic and ready to face the day, whatever it might bring. After a moment's indecision she replaced her bikini, but left off the skirt and blouse. She would dry off first, she decided, even if she were risking shocking the guard.

He regarded her as impassively as ever. Neil took the soap from her as she came in and signalled that he too wanted to wash. The guard locked her in the room and escorted Neil to the shower block in his turn, standing outside with his gun at the ready while Neil was inside.

'Back,' he ordered, gesturing with it towards the room. Obediently Neil made to go back, but once he was level with the door he stopped. He pointed first to the sun and then to his own wet skin. He added something in Chinese and made to sit down on the edge of the verandah, a move which caused the guard to shout and wave his gun about. Neil shrugged resignedly and stood up, waiting while the guard unlocked the door and pushed him inside.

'This is a ridiculous situation,' he said to Sue once they were alone. 'I could have broken away from him several times during that little excursion.'

'What about the gun? And, anyway, you said yourself there was nowhere to run to.'

'If only we knew where we were.' Neil ran his fingers through his hair. 'Maybe we're not far from Canton. I don't mean walking distance — obviously we're not that — but we could be within easy reach by train or by road. If they consistently stop us seeing someone in authority, maybe we should try to get there. At least there'd be a British consul there, I imagine. I get the feeling we could rot away here and no one would be any the wiser.'

'That is not what I call looking on the bright side.'

'Well, it's not exactly easy to find one, is it?'

'We're together,' Sue said stubbornly. Neil took her hand.

'That's the way it'll stay,' he said.

He was prevented from saying more by the reappearance of the guard. He seemed now to have had second thoughts about his refusal to let them sit outside, or else his orders had been changed. He gestured to them to sit on the verandah and gratefully they obeyed, welcoming a change from the confinement of the little room. He stationed himself at his usual vantage-point at the open end of the small square, sitting on the verandah of the last hut opposite to their prison, and watched them unblinkingly.

'What a strange place this is!' Neil mused, looking round him. 'It's derelict.'

'Our room isn't,' Sue reminded him. 'It's almost as if it had been repainted especially for us.'

Neil stood up and stretched. At his first movement, the guard stood up too and levelled his gun. Neil gave him a friendly wave and sat down again. The guard subsided.

'I'm sure I'm right about there being a village down that hill,' he said. 'Smiler is just coming up, pushing his bike, looking as if he's weighed down with groceries. I hope they're not getting in provisions for a long stay.'

'It seems odd that there are so few of them.'

'Very.' Neil looked around again. 'I suppose it's possible that there are other prisoners here,' he said. 'Or would we have heard them? I wonder if all these other rooms are empty.' He looked thoughtfully at the second door that gave on to their verandah, the door of the room next to theirs.

'I'd like to look in there.'

'I'm sure there's no one there.'

'Perhaps not — still, I'm curious. Sue, I want you to do something. Pretend to be ill — have a bad stomach-ache, double up with pain, anything to attract the guard's attention.'

'What are you planning?'

'Nothing much. Just a quick look.'

She took a deep breath. 'OK, here goes.' She gave a moan, which was totally ignored by the guard.

'Suffer, suffer,' urged Neil.

She shot him a dirty look, bent double and groaned again, much louder. This time the guard appeared to notice that something was wrong and stood up. Neil sprang to his feet and bent over her with concern as she groaned and rolled around in agony. He looked up towards the soldier and called him, indicating Sue. Talking to him, cajoling him to bring her some assistance, he walked to the far end of the verandah until the perplexed guard, not knowing quite what was going on, shouted at him to stay where he was. Sue's moans were subsiding a little by this time.

'Bring her some water,' Neil shouted. 'Can't you see she's ill?'

'You stay, you stay,' the guard ordered. He called for help and the smiling soldier who had been pushing his bike up the hill appeared round the end of the far hut. The two guards held a brief conference, after which the latest arrival scurried away to reappear in a short time with a mug of water.

Neil took it from him, effusive in his thanks. He turned round slowly to carry it back to Sue, now an inert and silent form lying on the verandah. As if anxious not to spill a drop, he hesitated and hoped it would not be noticed that this coincided with passing the window of the locked room next door. The guard shouted, but he was unaware of it as he continued on his way. On his face was an expression of complete incredulity.

Sue took the water and sagged against the wooden pillar supporting the verandah roof, doing her best to look pale and wan. She closed her eyes and panted weakly.

'You can recover,' Neil said. 'Nice and slowly. Smiler's gone and the other is sitting down again.'

There was a suppressed excitement in his voice that made her look at him searchingly.

'You saw something,' she said.

He sat down close beside her, his legs hanging over the edge of the verandah.

'You were right, it's empty. Just four, dirty, bare walls. Correction — they weren't quite bare. Someone had written a message on one of them.'

'Saying what?'

'Would you believe — would you *possibly* believe 'Everton for the Cup'?'

There was a moment of utter silence.

Then 'Everton for the — you mean it was in *English*?'

'Certainly was.'

'But it doesn't make sense! Why would Chinese soldiers . . . ' her voice trailed away. 'Do you think that other prisoners have been here, then?'

'Speaking personally as a prisoner, the

football scores are the last thing on my mind.'

'Then what?'

'Look Sue, it sounds fantastic — but just suppose for a moment that this isn't China at all: Suppose we're just being conned into thinking so, so that we won't try to escape. Suppose this is an abandoned British army post — there are quite a few about, now that the army is being run down out here. The whole thing makes sense then — why we were picked up in what I know were British waters, why this place is falling to pieces, why there isn't anyone in authority, why there's English graffiti on the walls.'

'Why one room only was painted, especially for us. Maybe that had something written on the walls too! But, Neil, it's only supposition, isn't it?'

'Another thing.' Neil shot a glance at the guard, afraid that the exuberance in his voice would carry. He was reassured by the sight of the soldier looking aimlessly out over the patch between the huts. 'When Smiler came up the hill, pushing his bike, he was on the left side, wasn't he? And in China they drive on the right.'

'Are you sure?'

'Certain.'

'But the boat, Neil, and the flag. And the uniforms! Surely they're authentic.'

'A Hong Kong tailor could run them up in hours. And the boat only looked official because it was painted grey. They probably relied on us being too shocked to notice much about it.'

'But *why*, Neil?'

'I don't know.' He was silent for a moment. 'Maybe Edward ratted to his father after all. Perhaps this is just a complicated way of getting rid of us.'

'Why not just shoot us and put us over the side?'

'If it's anything to do with Wong there has to be a profit motive.'

'Kidnap?'

Neil looked at her. 'I wouldn't be surprised if you'd guessed it.' He thought it over. 'Yes, I rather like it. It explains why nothing's happened yet. They're keeping us on ice until someone pays a ransom.'

Sue thought this over. 'And then do you think they'll let us go?'

'You must be joking! Somehow we've got to get out, Sue — before any money changes hands. We'll have to think this over very carefully. We may only have one chance, so we mustn't make a mess of it.' Neil was silent for a moment, his thoughts racing furiously.

'We'd have to get him in the room

somehow — the guard, I mean, and silence him quickly.'

'How?'

'I'm working on it. What we need is a blunt instrument and something to tie him up with afterwards.' They were both silent, thinking of their limited resources.

'There's wire in the loo,' Sue said. 'You know, instead of a chain.'

'So there is. Right — that's one problem solved. But what do we knock the bastard out with?'

'If you had a sock,' Sue said helpfully, 'you could fill it with sand. If we had any sand.'

'I'll file the suggestion for the next, similar occasion. Any other bright ideas?'

She looked round the bare patch of earth, relieved only by the scrawny tree in the centre bed, and shook her head slowly.

'Nothing strikes me. Can you take the bed to pieces?'

'I don't think so. Sue, I think I've got it.'

'What?'

'See the tree over there? It's in a circular bed, edged with bricks, right?' Sue nodded.

'One of those bricks would be just dandy. Now how the hell do I get hold of one?'

'Ask him if we can walk around here.'

'You're supposed to be ill!'

'The exercise will do me good. If we just

keep on walking, he'll get tired of watching us. You can take your shirt off to get the maximum effect of the beneficial rays of the sun, and with any luck you might be able to whip one of the bricks underneath it. It all sounds very simple to me.'

'Well, it's worth a try.'

As on other occasions, the guard objected violently at first when exercise was suggested, but then changed his mind. On the face of it, it seemed an innocent enough pastime. They walked round and round in a small, circumscribed area and, as they hoped, the guard shortly lost interest. Neil loosened a brick with his foot each time they passed it, but it was not until a second guard appeared with a tray of food and stopped for a brief word with his mate that he felt safe enough to pick up the brick and secreted it quickly under his shirt.

They were once more herded into the room and the door was locked. 'This is what we'll do,' said Neil and began to lay out his plans.

The long afternoon eventually began to fade. They had lain close together throughout the hours of waiting, talking of everything except their escape. This they had gone over in the smallest detail earlier and both knew the part they were to play. Now Neil went over to the window. Sue raised herself from the pillow and watched him.

'Do you know where to go, once we're out?'

'I know which way's west. If this is the New Territories, that should do to be going on with.'

'What's the time?'

'Ten past six. They'll be bringing our supper soon.'

Sue groaned. 'More rice! I don't know if I can stand it.'

'With luck, Serena will be cooking you a nice juicy steak in a few hours.'

'Don't tempt providence!'

The evening followed the routine set the day before. The meal was brought and they ate as much as they could stomach, drinking the green tea gratefully. It was almost dark by the time they had finished and the guard arrived to escort them to the shower-block. As they had arranged, Sue went first and was back quickly. Then it was Neil's turn.

To Sue, waiting impatiently in the room, he seemed to be gone an age. She heard the guard shouting at him, banging on the door. Every nerve in her body was keyed to the highest pitch and she leant against the wall by the door, hands to her mouth. Maybe that wire wasn't so easy to detach as they had imagined. It had obviously been there a long time, replacing the chain, and could well have rusted to the point where it was impossible to remove with bare hands.

At last she heard two pairs of footsteps returning. The room was shadowy, but outside it was not fully dark. As the door opened she saw that Neil was smiling.

'OK,' he said, and she went into action.

'Look over here,' she said, pretending great agitation and pulling the guard over towards the second bed. 'There's a snake. Very big. Very dangerous.'

Obligingly Neil supplied the Cantonese word and the guard repeated it in a horrified voice. Very gingerly he bent down, peering beneath the bed.

Neil was only a few paces behind, the brick in his hand. The guard turned to straighten up and received the full force of it on the front of his head. With a dull thud he dropped to the ground.

'Oh, the poor little man,' Sue whispered. 'You haven't killed him, have you?'

'Not a chance.' Grimly Neil was folding the guard up as if in a parcel, wiring his wrists and ankles firmly together. He gagged him with a strip torn from a blanket.

'That should at least slow him down. OK, then? All set?'

Silently he went to the door and looked out. It was much darker now and the road leading from the cluster of huts showed white amid the shadows. There was no sign of the other guards. Either they were in another part of the camp, Neil thought, or down in the village for the evening. Carefully he padlocked the door behind them, and silent as shadows they moved along the verandah towards the road.

The hill that was revealed in front of them was steep. Almost directly below the village soon became visible. They could see isolated lights.

A stream rushed and gurgled somewhere to their left and to the right was steep hillside, thickly wooded. Neil, remembering the difficulty of their approach to the camp, resolved to keep well away from it.

The track ahead of them was empty, but the shadows cast by trees played strange tricks as the wind stirred the branches. A dozen times Sue's heart tripped and she prepared to drop into the ditch, only to find that it was an innocent tree-stump or a waving bough that had startled her. Neil walked fractionally ahead of her, but her hand was in his and she marvelled at the sense of security this gave her. Blindly she trusted him to get them both out of this mess.

He stopped in his tracks and Sue caught her breath. They had rounded a bend in the road and could now see lights ahead of them. There was some sort of road junction there. As they watched, pressing back into the trees, a car passed along the road at the top and Neil squeezed her hand.

'See that?' he whispered. 'A Ford Cortina, no less. We're in British territory, all right.'

'Would they help us?'

'No — the two other guards must be down there somewhere. There's probably a bar. I think this is where we take to the woods.'

Another yard, and they had found a small track leading into the trees. Trailing plants caught at their feet and thick foliage impeded their way, but only for a short distance. Neil exclaimed softly as they chanced upon a more clearly defined path, edged with stones, which seemed to lead towards the river.

'Civilisation!' commented Sue, pointing to a litter-bin.

'Look.' Neil pointed upwards. Nailed to a tree and only dimly visible was a rustic notice on which, in white letters, were painted the words 'Picnic Site': An arrow pointed along the path and following its direction they found themselves in a clearing where the stream tumbled over rocks to make a small waterfall. Strategically placed under the surrounding trees were rustic tables and benches, with barbecue pits beside them.

Neil looked round uneasily.

'I'm going to leave you for a moment, but not here,' he said. 'Anyone could come.'

'At night?'

'Kids have barbecues at night — or maybe some of those lovers we mentioned the other day might be looking for a bit of seclusion. Look, come over by this tree. Merge into the shadows. That's fine.'

'Where are you going?'

'Just to spy out the land. If anyone comes, freeze.'

Unhappily, hating to be left alone, Sue watched him go. All too soon he was swallowed up by the darkness and the woodland was silent — or so she thought at first. Then she became aware of a medley of night noises, of rustles and squeaks and a strangely insistent piping that could have been a bird, yet was unlike any bird she had ever heard. Something crawled over her foot and she slapped it away, feeling hysteria rising. She closed her eyes, willing herself to be calm. In a few minutes Neil would be back.

A twig snapped close to her and her eyes flew open. Could he possibly be back so soon? She clenched her teeth to keep from screaming as a bat swooped close to her face; she could feel the rush of air as it passed and her skin crawled.

Someone was in the clearing. Neil? No, not possibly. This person had a torch and seemed to be searching for something, the light bobbing this way and that. As he came nearer, Sue could see he was a strange, bent figure with rags for clothes. At one point he directed the beam upwards so that his head was clearly illuminated, a sight that made her catch her breath in horror, for he was a fearsome, unearthly sight with wild matted hair, his eyes fixed and staring. He was looking on the ground now, bending low, the beam of his torch going this way and that. Sue edged silently round the tree-trunk away from him, feeling sure that any moment he would light up her sandalled feet. She leaned against the tree, careless now of the insects that would crawl over her. Nothing was more frightening than this weird creature who looked as if he had come straight from hell.

His search seemed endless, but eventually she was aware that he had gone. The clearing was left to the night creatures again and the thudding of her own heart.

Neil suddenly materialised beside her and

wordlessly she clung to him, half-sobbing.

'It's all right! Darling, it's all right, I promise. He's gone.'

She took a deep and shuddering breath. 'Who was he, Neil? He looked like a monster.'

'He was just a beggar — a tramp, looking for food left by the picnickers, I suppose. I was watching from the other side of the clearing. He was probably harmless.'

'He didn't look it.'

'No — but forget him, darling. I've got some really good news — news you'll hardly believe.'

'Try me.'

He pointed across the clearing. 'Just down there, if we follow the path, we come to the main road. And guess what? Right at the end of the path there's a bus-stop. There's an old girl waiting there and I spun her a yarn about going for a walk and getting lost and asked her about buses. Darling, there's one to the Star Ferry in five minutes!'

Weakly Sue dropped her head against his shoulder and began to laugh softly. 'You're right — I don't believe it! You can't just walk out of prison and catch a bus.'

'Shh!' Neil said cautiously, but he was laughing too. 'Imagine thinking we were in China when we were only a bus-ride away from Kowloon. Just a dollar fare away from freedom.'

'It's unbelievable.' She straightened up and smoothed her hair. 'We haven't much time to waste then. Maybe we should join the queue.'

11

For the first time in her own or anyone else's memory, Marsha Wong stayed away from her salon on Monday morning. The Chinese are an industrious race at the best of times. Marsha took this natural industry to extremes, driven on day after day by a never-diminishing need to exploit her own efficiency and flair for fashion. She often thought that she would find it impossible to retire, even when she was old.

But this day was different. She had woken with an unbearable feeling of lethargy and malaise which made it impossible for her to face the day. She had an interview arranged with a buyer. She had promised to phone a fashion house in Rome. There was new stock to be priced, staff problems to be settled. All this would have to wait. She could think of nothing but Sue.

Where *was* Sue? She had phoned her the day before to tell her of the meeting she had arranged with the technician who would make the jewellery. Nothing more had been said by Paul and she considered it best to continue her life as if nothing had happened

— to go ahead with her plans with Sue. But Sue was not at home and there had been something strange in Ian's voice when he had told her his sister was away for a few days.

The more she thought about it, the more convinced she became that something had happened to her. At first she had taken Paul's word that the house in Deepwater bay would be closed down at its face value — but Kee had gone away whistling that night and Paul had been altogether too cheerful for a man who was about to lose a substantial income.

Only Sue and Neil Marriner stood between Paul and the uninterrupted pursuit of his lucrative business. Others had been killed for no more. This was the thought that beat inside her head, making her feel as if it would explode — for this time she felt certain that he would not get away with it.

Perhaps Paul felt the same, for his cheerfulness — totally unexpected after that awful night when he had discovered that she had told Sue about the bracelet — had suddenly turned to anger again last night after a phone call. He did not tell her who had called or what message he had been given, but he had shut himself in the library and kept the phone busy himself for the best part of the evening. Such was his black rage over what had happened, whatever it might be, that she kept well away from him.

Something had happened to Sue. She knew it as surely as she knew that the sun would rise over the mountains towards China and the knowledge filled her with a sickening dread. She phoned the salon to say she was ill, ordered more coffee and crawled back to bed, suddenly feeling her age. Doesn't there come a time for peace in our lives? she asked herself. Doesn't the running ever stop?

Edward's life would be different. She didn't understand him and she knew that he despised her, but he was young and he would surely forget his extremist views as time went by. Eventually he would settle down to being a hardworking, industrious citizen on the right side of the law. She was thankful that so far he wanted nothing to do with the Triads. Yes, it would all be different for him.

Perhaps, as Sue had said, he would find himself at Oxford. His bags were packed and labelled in his room. He had some last-minute shopping to do, he said, but would be back in plenty of time to get to the airport. It had sounded almost as if he were getting excited at the thought. She would be glad to see him go. It would be one less thing to worry about, if there was to be trouble . . . if Paul were to be . . . A shutter fell over her mind. It was too horrible to imagine. She had to curb her thoughts before they drove her mad.

At lunch-time she roused herself and went downstairs. Edward was standing in the window of the sitting-room looking out over the bay, the usual closed expression on his face.

'All ready?' she asked.

'More or less,' he answered without turning round and Marsha looked at him sadly, biting her lip.

'You know we wish you well,' she said.

He turned and faced her, a slight smile on his thin lips. He inclined his head politely, as if to a stranger.

'I wish — I wish — ' Marsha gestured helplessly.

He turned back to contemplating the garden. 'I think we all wish a lot of things.'

'It would be nice if we could talk.'

He took a deep, exasperated breath. 'There's nothing to say.'

'We always wanted the best for you, your father and I.'

'I know, Mother.' He turned to face her again and for a moment she thought that he was going to say more. Words seemed to tremble on his lips, but the gulf between them was too great and no words existed that could bridge it. He began to walk towards the door.

'Don't go, Edward. What about lunch?' Marsha's voice held a desperate plea, but Edward ignored it.

'I'm sorry, Mother,' he said and left the room.

Summoned by Ying, Marsha toyed with her lunch alone at the vast table in the dining-room. Her head ached intolerably and she could hardly bring herself to answer Ying who was full of queries about fish. Fish? Who on earth cared about fish?

'Do what you think best,' she said irritably.

She waved away most of the food, leaving the amah resentfully clearing away the half-eaten meal and muttering under her breath. She went upstairs and into her bathroom, reaching for the aspirin and washing them down with water from the tap. She took off her dress and lay down on her bed, her sleepless nights catching up on her at last. She would feel better after a sleep, she told herself. Perhaps things would look different if she were not so tired.

The telephone bell shrilled through her dreams and for a moment she found it hard to remember where she was or what time of day it was. Of course, it was afternoon; she had taken aspirin and slept, and now she was awake and her headache was as bad as ever. She groped for the phone by the bed, but even as her fingers found it the bell stopped; someone had answered it downstairs. She lifted the receiver anyway. Ying was quite useless at taking messages and inevitably they were garbled.

It was not Ying's voice that she heard, however. The call, it seemed, had been for Edward and curiously she listened, knowing so little of his friends and desperate to know more.

'Surprised to hear from me?' she heard. She frowned. The voice was somehow familiar but she could not put a name to it. An English voice, that was certain.

'Why should I be?' Edward replied.

'Then our meeting is going through as arranged?' The unknown caller hesitated a moment. 'I wondered if everything was still OK.'

'As far as I'm aware — but you shouldn't have phoned me here.'

'Sorry. Just checking. I'll see you on the beach in twenty minutes, then. Over and out.'

'Wait!' Edward's voice sounded agitated. 'Marriner, wait.'

'Yes?'

'If there are any complications, you owe it to me to tell me. I'm laying myself wide open by giving you the evidence — '

'Just shut up and get on with it, mate.

There aren't any complications, but there sure as hell will be if you're not here in twenty minutes. Understood?'

The phone went dead and gently Marsha replaced her receiver. Evidence, Edward had said. What could he mean? Her head throbbed and for a moment she buried it in her hands desperately trying to make sense of the conversation she had overheard. Only one thing was clear. Neil Marriner was Paul's enemy.

She threw off the light cover and rushed to the wardrobe, hastily zipping herself into her dress and tying the belt as she fumbled for her shoes and made for the door. As she reached the top of the stairs she saw Edward coming out of the library and into the hall, several books under his arm. She called to him and for an instant his colourless, set face was turned towards her, then he had wrenched at the front door, opened it and slammed it behind him.

Marsha ran down the stairs and into the library, knowing what she would find, yet aghast at the sight that met her eyes. The door of the safe was wide open and the account-books were gone.

She moaned softly, knowing how incriminating they would be in the wrong hands, even though she had never actually studied them herself. They had to be incriminating for Paul to keep them like this, apart from everything else.

In a split second she was out of the room, out of the house and down the steps. Edward had already backed his car out of the garage and was almost at the end of the drive. She could see him waiting there by the gates for a break in the traffic and prayed that the wait would be as prolonged as it often was on a fine summer afternoon, with scores of cars heading to and from the beach.

She ran to the garage and leapt into her own car, only a minute behind him, but he had seized his opportunity and was off, down the road towards the bay. Marsha roared up the drive and after him, swerving right in the face of an oncoming bus. There was a screech of brakes, but miraculously she was clear, totally unaware of the hostile and curious glances she was exciting from other motorists. She could see the yellow of Edward's Mini-Cooper ahead of her, with only one car between them. There was no room to pass — no room at all — but somehow she did so, flying with only a millimetre to spare between herself, the intervening car and a taxi coming in the opposite direction.

Still Edward was ahead of her. The traffic thickened as they approached the beach. Cars were parked at the side of the road and pedestrians ambled across to buy hamburgers and ice-creams. Marsha, hands gripping the wheel until the knuckles were white, saw no one. The only reality was the little yellow car ahead and her only aim to prevent Edward passing the incriminating books to Neil Marriner.

The mini slid into a small parking-place. She was forced to stop several yards behind it as a station-wagon filled with children and beach-balls and rubber rings pulled out in front of her and with a frustration that reduced her almost to tears she saw Edward get out of his car and hurry across to the beach. She flicked a look across. She could see no one that looked like Neil Marriner, but there were so many people, both Chinese and European. He could be anywhere.

The station-wagon had finally gone and she drove into the space it had vacated, clumsily and carelessly. There was no time to straighten the car. One wheel was on the pavement and the tail was out so far that oncoming traffic slowed and hooted as it approached, but there was no time to improve on it. She got out of the car and slammed the door. Now she could see Neil Marriner. He was sitting under the canopy of the café at a wooden table. Edward had spotted him too and was going across to him.

She shouted wildly and started across the road, turning in fury as someone caught hold of her arm. It was a policeman, mouthing inanities and gesturing at the car. She understood not a word. Nothing mattered but getting to Edward before he reached Marriner and with superhuman strength she shook the man away, turning to rush blindly across the road.

'Edward,' she shrieked. 'Edward, for the love of God — '

The sports car, driven much too fast, was on her before she saw it. The policeman stood in open-mouthed horror as she was mown down before his eyes and there was an orchestrated gasp from the bystanders.

Edward, ploughing across the beach with his back to the road, saw nothing. Neil took the books and documents from him.

'That's everything?' he asked.

'Everything.'

'Thanks. I'm very grateful.'

'You won't do anything with them until after I've gone.'

Neil hesitated. 'I did promise, didn't I? But see here, Edward — the position has changed somewhat. You don't know about your father's attempt at abduction, I take it?'

'What on earth do you mean?'

Neil gestured dismissively. 'Never mind — leave it. It's too long to go into now. The fact remains that I — and others — are in danger while your father is free. What time's take-off?'

'Seven-thirty.'

'Then pray the plane leaves on time, because that's the longest I'm prepared to wait. After that, come hell or high water, fire, flood or typhoon, those documents go to the authorities. Understood?'

Edward said nothing, recognising the fact that now the evidence was out of his hands there was nothing that could be said. He watched silently as Neil locked the books into his brief-case and it was only then that he turned and they both became aware that there had been an accident on the road behind them.

'Some idiot not looking where he was going,' Edward said, without sympathy.

It was only afterwards that Neil remembered the remark and wondered if, after all, it had not been a rather neat epitaph for Marsha Wong.

He left Edward and struck off along the beach at right angles, only half-believing that the evidence was there in his hand. An incredulous exultation grew inside him, making him want to shout aloud in triumph.

Paul Wong's arrest was now certain. It would only be a matter of hours.

There was, however, still a short time to get through, as a small and cautious inward voice reminded him. Wong's men would undoubtedly be looking for him and for Sue too. He was hardly likely to sit by resignedly once he had learned they had escaped from the camp in the New Territories.

Here, on the beach among so many others, there was a feeling of safety. He threaded his way between families and groups of young people, keeping a watchful eye open for anyone who might seem interested in his progress.

Cutting up to the road close to the lido he heard a shout, but ignored it, intent now on getting to his car and back to Sue as quickly as possible. He felt someone grip his shoulder and he turned, the hand holding the briefcase drawn back to land a savage blow, his mouth rigid with desperation.

Ian Russell dropped his arm and stepped back, hands raised in an attitude of surrender.

'I say, steady on, old chap! I didn't mean to startle you.'

Neil stood for a moment, transfixed, then slowly let out his breath.

'You were bloody nearly clobbered there,

mate. What was the idea of creeping up on me like that?'

'Creeping is hardly the word! I've been pounding along the road after you from way back — would have caught you earlier but there's been some sort of accident on the road and the police wouldn't let the car pass. I sent it back to the office with the driver — thought I'd get a lift with you.'

'But what are you doing here?'

'Following you, what else? That sister of mine rang me up, apparently demented with worry. Either I came to keep an eye on you or she would, she said. I didn't have a lot of choice, did I? Where are you parked?'

'Somewhere where Wong's boys wouldn't find the car, if they were out looking for it. I ran it into the garage of a friend of mine who lives up the road.'

They fell into step together and Ian nodded at the brief-case.

'There was no trouble, then? You got everything you wanted.'

'Yes, this is the lot.' He laughed a little. 'What on earth did Sue think she could do, I wonder — or you, for that matter — if Wong had located me and sent the heavies in?'

'Women aren't exactly logical when they're in love.'

Neil looked at him sideways at this.

'How do you feel about that particular situation?'

'I'm pleased. Just don't hurt her, will you?'

'Never in a million years,' Neil promised.

They reached the car and eased out into the traffic on the main road, joining the slow moving tail-back that had been caused by the arrival of the ambulance and the clearing away of the cars involved in the accident. Neil fumed, beating his hands on the wheel in his impatience. Eventually they reached and edged past the mangled sports car that had swerved and ploughed into the other cars at the side of the road.

'What a mess!' he said. 'I'll bet whoever was involved with that didn't come out alive.'

'I wonder,' Ian remarked at precisely that moment, 'how involved Marsha Wong was in this racket? Do you think she'll get off?'

'Heaven knows.' Neil accelerated now that the traffic was flowing freely again. 'She must have known about it and she certainly profited by the proceeds — but maybe she'll be able to squirm out of it somehow. Whatever happens, it will be a thoroughly nasty business.

'I'll be thankful when the whole thing is tied up,' Ian said. 'Neither you nor Sue will be safe until it is.'

'I'm only too well aware of that.' Neil

gritted his teeth with annoyance as the traffic slowed to a halt again. 'Oh, come *on*! For God's sake, get a move on. I don't like the thought of those two girls up there on their own.'

'Hardly on their own, with armed police outside the front gate. They'll surely be safe.'

Neil gave a short laugh. 'Well, you know how it is,' he said. 'Men aren't exactly logical when they're in love.'

★   ★   ★

Sue and Serena were in the sitting-room. Sue had been attempting to read and Serena had brought out some long-neglected petit point, but the appearance of restful ease was misleading. For the fiftieth time Sue put her book down and sighed gustily.

'Oh, where are they?' she asked. 'It's time they were back.'

'Relax, Sue. You know what the traffic is like at this time of day.'

'I keep thinking, I wish he'd taken a police escort with him. I know he promised Edward it would all be secret, but that was before the kidnapping. If it was necessary for me to be guarded, it must be just as necessary for him.'

'Ian went after him.'

'I know.' Sue gave the ghost of a grin. 'I

mean no disrespect to my dear brother, whom I love with a passion, but what could he do against Wong's thugs? They're a desperate lot, Serena.'

'He could raise the alarm.' Serena put her petit point on one side. 'Do you know what I'm going to do? I'm going to get us both a large brandy — strictly for medicinal purposes. No, no arguments! I am well aware that the sun isn't over the yardarm, but the times are unusual.'

'Listen.' Sue raised her head. 'That's a car, isn't it?' She got to her feet, then sagged with disappointment. 'No, it's not. At least, it's not coming to the front.'

'It was probably on the road.' Serena was on her feet too, on her way to the drinks cabinet, but she stopped in her tracks, her head tilted. 'What on earth's going on in the kitchen?'

The sound of raised voices came to them quite clearly, even though the kitchen was at the far end of the house. Serena went out into the passage, brandy decanter in hand, and after standing for a moment, a puzzled expression on her face, followed the sound of the voices to their source. Sue, sensing trouble, was not far behind.

They found Ah Moy standing as if at bay in the middle of the room shouting at a white-uniformed Chinese who was holding a large cardboard carton in his arms, piled with groceries. She turned defensively as she heard Serena behind her.

'Missee, you tell me no one must come in. You say police stop people at gate.'

'It's only your groceries, Madam.' The delivery-man held out a bill, with its familiar lay-out and logo clearly visible. A smart Dairy Farm van was drawn up outside the back door.

Serena looked uncertain. 'It's not your normal day, surely?'

The delivery-man was young with a round, cheerful face. He smiled at Serena.

'Later this week, I go holiday. Bling your things today.'

'Oh, all right — put them down anywhere.'

She waved her hand vaguely at the expanse of yellow formica and turned to leave the kitchen, but a sharp yelp from Ah Moy made her jerk round quickly. The box of groceries was down on the kitchen table and in the hand of the cheerful delivery-man was a snub-nosed gun.

For a moment it was as if they were frozen into immobility, a macabre tableau. Then Serena screamed and hurled the decanter at the man, knocking him a little off balance and giving them time to turn and run.

'Outside, Sue,' Serena yelled and both girls took off down the passage and into the sitting-room with the intention of getting out to the terrace, from where they hoped to make their way to the front of the house and thence to the gate, where the police were supposed to be guarding them.

Breath sobbing in their throats, they ran through the room and out of the long windows, turning left to circle the house. But before they could reach the corner a second gunman ran round it towards them — the man who had been at the wheel of the delivery-van. He raised his gun to fire at Sue, who was slightly in the lead, but without slackening her stride she had changed course, obeying Serena's shrieked instructions to go down the steps towards the pool.

A bullet whistled past over their heads. Where the hell were the police? Sue wondered, screaming for help at the top of her voice. Surely they had to hear them. The drive wasn't all that long, the gate not so far distant. Where were they heading? Did Serena have some idea of reaching the next garden and the safety of neighbours? Surely *someone* had to hear them! Coherent thought was impossible. It was instinct now, a fight for survival, a nightmare flight with both assailants only feet behind them.

It had been a mistake to come outside. At least in the house they could have locked themselves in a room, have telephoned for help, have done a thousand things to defend themselves.

Sue glanced over her shoulder and screamed again as she saw the grinning face of the driver-turned-gunman close behind her. He reached out a hand and grasped her dress which tore as she flung herself away from him. The chase was over though. It could only be a matter of seconds now. An arm pinioned her from behind and the gun rammed against her temple. He shouted an order to Serena who stopped in her headlong flight down the stone steps, looking back in horror.

'No, no,' she moaned softly, gasping for breath. 'Don't shoot her. Please don't shoot her.'

The man threw Sue away from him so that she stumbled down the remaining few steps and was caught by Serena.

'Stay together,' he ordered. 'There, close to the wall.'

'Don't shoot,' Serena whispered again.

The pleasant-faced delivery-boy squeezed past the driver on the steps and came to stand in front of them.

'So solly, Mrs Lussell,' he said, smiling still. 'We have our orders.'

*   *   *

'This *bloody* traffic!' Neil wound down his window and the blast of hot air surging into the air-conditioned interior of the car made him wince. He leaned out to look along the line of traffic to see if there was anything in particular holding them up, but shook his head as he would the window up again. 'It's nothing,' he said. 'Just the usual rush-hour build up.'

'There are times when one longs for a six-lane motorway.'

'You're not kidding: I swear this car hasn't been in top gear more than a handful of times in the whole of its life. Thank heaven, we appear to be moving again.'

They turned left towards the Peak and, although the winding road made high speed impossible, at least the traffic was moving. Neil breathed a sigh of relief as he passed the Peak tram terminus and turned up the hill still further. Now he could see the wrought-iron gates of the Russell residence ahead of him. A police car was parked outside and Neil slowed down, winding his window down again as he drew opposite. He frowned as he realised that loud pop music was filling the air. The policemen had found waiting tedious, it seemed.

'No trouble?' he asked, when they had turned the music down sufficiently for him to make himself heard.

'No tlouble, sir.'

'Turn that damned racket off. You wouldn't hear if anything did happen.'

'Nothing happen, sir. No one come. Only Dairy Farm.'

'*What?* You were told to let no one — ' he broke off as the dishevelled figure of Ah Moy came running up the drive. He made to leap out to open the gates, but Ian was there before him. The cascade of Cantonese that poured from her lips was impossible to understand, but Neil did not wait to be enlightened. In any language, Ah Moy was quite obviously frightened out of her wits.

'Follow me,' he yelled to the police and took off down the drive, Ian jumping in and hanging on to the still-open door as Neil, his foot hard on the accelerator, roared towards the house. He switched off the engine and in the silence that followed they both heard the despairing cry for help.

'It came from outside,' Ian shouted. 'You go that way, I'll go this.'

From opposite directions they ran round the house, both closely followed by a policeman, their guns already out of their holsters. They converged on the terrace at the front of the house and registered with horror the drama that was about to be enacted down by the pool.

Suddenly masters of the situation, the police took over and Neil almost forgave them their previous negligence, it was in such a professional way they dealt with the gunmen below. They were down the steps almost before his brain had time to register the fact and with their guns raised had ordered the men to throw down their weapons.

Suddenly it was all over. Sue and Serena clung together while the gunmen were handcuffed, until Neil and Ian appeared beside them, when they changed partners and clung to their respective men.

'You were *told* not to let anyone in,' Ian said afterwards. He and Serena were occupying one large chair, while Sue and Neil sat close together on the settee.

'It happened before we knew it,' Serena explained. 'Honestly, they looked so genuine. Even the police were fooled, after all.'

'If those policemen hadn't acted so well at the end, they'd be in dead trouble.' Neil held

Sue close at the thought of what so nearly had happened. 'Didn't they enjoy it though? All those weeks of watching Starsky and Hutch weren't wasted after all.'

'How's Ah Moy?' Sue asked. 'Has she recovered?'

'I think so, bless her heart. They locked her in the store, did you know? But she smashed a window and managed to get out.'

Ian extricated himself from the chair.

'That reminds me. I must make sure that window's blocked up again. Apart from that, I think this house is pretty impregnable — and I'm personally going to see it stays that way until Wong's behind bars.'

Neil looked at his watch, sighed and restlessly got up to move over to the window.

'This time-limit is absurd,' he said. 'I should never have agreed to it.'

'You'd never have got the evidence from Edward without it.'

'That's true.' He turned to smile at Sue as she joined him by the window, reaching out to draw her to him with an arm around her shoulders. His smile died as once more he turned his gaze back to the city below them; that fascinating, beautiful, infuriating, oppressive, exhilarating, contradictory place that was Hong Kong.

'If seven maids with seven mops, swept

for half a year . . . '

He spoke quietly and ruefully, more to himself than to anyone else.

'At least one small corner of it is likely to be a little less corrupt when Paul Wong is taken care of,' Sue said.

'I guess. You know what they say, don't you? A borrowed place, living on borrowed time . . . '

'Well, this is one debt that's going to be paid. The debt to Mali.'

'How many other Malis are out there? How many Wongs? How much corruption?'

'That's only one side of it. There's beauty too, and you know it. And vitality and colour and excitement.'

Neil looked down at her, smiling again.

'Reckon you'll stay, then?'

She laughed back at him.

'Play your cards right!'

'It's time, Neil.' Ian's voice interrupted them from across the room. 'Do you want me to come with you?'

'I'd be happier to know you were here, thanks all the same.'

In spite of his former hurry to be gone, he made no move to leave Sue, turning to face her with his hands on her shoulders. For a moment he studied her face without speaking, then gave her a small shake.

'Stick around, do you hear?' he said. 'I shan't be long.'

And, picking up the brief-case, he left the room.

THE END

We do hope that you have enjoyed reading this large print book.

Did you know that all of our titles are available for purchase?

We publish a wide range of high quality large print books including:
Romances, Mysteries, Classics
General Fiction
Non Fiction and Westerns

Special interest titles available in large print are:
The Little Oxford Dictionary
Music Book
Song Book
Hymn Book
Service Book

Also available from us courtesy of Oxford University Press:
Young Readers' Dictionary
(large print edition)
Young Readers' Thesaurus
(large print edition)

For further information or a free brochure, please contact us at:
Ulverscroft Large Print Books Ltd.,
The Green, Bradgate Road, Anstey,
Leicester, LE7 7FU, England.
Tel: (00 44) 0116 236 4325
Fax: (00 44) 0116 234 0205

Other titles in the
Ulverscroft Large Print Series:

THE FROZEN CEILING

Rona Randall

When Tessa Pickard found the note amongst her father's possessions, instinct told her that THIS had been responsible for his suicide, not the professional disgrace which had ruined his career as a mountaineer and instructor. The note was cryptic, anonymous, and bore a Norwegian postmark. Tessa promptly set out for Norway, determined to trace the anonymous letter-writer, but unprepared for the drama she was to uncover — or that compelling Max Hyerdal, whom she met on board a Norwegian ship, was to change her whole life.

GHOSTMAN

Kenneth Royce

Jones boasted that he never forgot a face. When he was found dead outside the National Gallery it was assumed he had remembered one too many. The man he had claimed to have identified had been publicly executed in Moscow some years before. The presumed look-alike was called Mirek and his background stood up. The Security Service calls in Willie 'Glasshouse' Jackson — Jacko — as they realise that there is a more sinister aspect. Jacko and his assistant begin to unearth commercial and political corruption in which life is cheap and profits vast, as the killing machines swing into action.

THE READER

Bernhard Schlink

A schoolboy in post-war Germany, Michael collapses one day in the street and is helped home by a woman in her thirties. He is fascinated by this older woman, and he and Hanna begin a secretive affair. Gradually, he begins to be frustrated by their relationship, but then is shocked when Hanna simply disappears. Some years later, as a law student, Michael is in court to follow a case. To his amazement he recognizes Hanna. The object of his adolescent passion is a criminal. Suddenly, Michael understands that her behaviour, both now and in the past, conceals a deeply buried secret.

THE WAY OF THE SEA AND OTHER STORIES

Stanley Wilson

Every story in this collection was written by Stanley Wilson with radio in mind. The BBC has broadcast all of them, and many have been used overseas. All have appeared in magazines or newspapers. The stories range the globe and beyond, from India to Canadian backwoods, from an expedition up the Amazon to a hundred years' journey to the planet Eithnan, from the Caribbean to a rain-sodden English seaside promenade, and from a fishing trawler to a hospital ward. There is frustration, there is tenderness, there is horror, there are tears, but there is laughter as well.

A BRIDE FOR
SIR BERENGAR LE MOYNE

Dora Woodhams

In 1258, seventeen-year-old Emma is faced with a dilemma: Her father is dying. He has sent for a comrade in arms, Sir Berengar le Moyne, to marry Emma if she agrees — and take her to his demesne of Bernewelle le Moyne, where she will be safe from the plots of her older half-brother Gerold, who plans to marry her to his only friend Sir Mauger when his father dies. Emma's eventual decision leads her into meeting King Henry III, his Queen, Eleanor of Provence, and Henry's son and his young bride, at the Royal Hunting Palace in Rockingham Forest.